A GALLANT COMPANY

EDITED BY

A. J. MERSON, M.A.
Headmaster, Carrick Academy, Maybole

LONGMANS, GREEN AND CO.

LONDON · NEW YORK · TORONTO

LONGMANS, GREEN AND CO. LTD.
39 PATERNOSTER ROW, LONDON, E.C.4
17 CHITTARANJAN AVENUE, CALCUTTA
NICOL ROAD, BOMBAY
36A MOUNT ROAD, MADRAS

LONGMANS, GREEN AND CO.
114 FIFTH AVENUE, NEW YORK
221 EAST 20TH STREET, CHICAGO
88 TREMONT STREET, BOSTON

LONGMANS, GREEN AND CO.
215 VICTORIA STREET, TORONTO

First published 1938

PRINTED IN GREAT BRITAIN BY
NORTHUMBERLAND PRESS LIMITED
GATESHEAD UPON TYNE

FOREWORD

LITTLE more than a century is represented by the authors from whose works the contents of this volume are taken, for Scott, who published the first of the Waverley Novels in 1814, died in 1832, while D. W. Bone and P. C. Wren are still with us. Yet, short as the period is, it covers the lives of the great writers who gave us our historical novels, romantic tales, and stories of adventure, and it is from among the characters they created that our " gallant company " has been chosen.

The impulse towards this kind of writing shows no sign of lessening vigour, nor have tales of this type lost any of their popularity and appeal. So in these pages you will find some of the greatest exponents, Scott, Dumas, Dickens, Stevenson, rubbing shoulders with writers of our own time whose names are less well known but whose writings worthily carry on the tradition. To be " gallant," you will find, is no prerogative of rank or race, or indeed of sex, and you will recognize in the heroes of the following tales a quality that lifts them out of the ordinary, a quality that can be felt rather than defined, but that seems to consist of varying proportions of courage, rashness, coolness, and that fundamental generosity of feeling, the possessor of which is described in schoolboy language as a " good sort."

But, whether renewing old friendships or making new ones, you are sure to enjoy these stories and to look forward to reading more by the same authors.

CONTENTS

ACKNOWLEDGMENTS

For permission to use copyright material I am indebted to the following:

The Executors of the late Mr. J. J. Bell for " The First Shot " from *The Whale Hunters*, published by Messrs. Hodder & Stoughton Ltd.; Messrs. Gerald Duckworth & Co. Ltd. for a chapter from *The Brassbounder* by Captain Bone; Lady Haggard for a passage from *Eric Brighteyes* by Sir H. Rider Haggard, published by Messrs. Longmans, Green & Co. Ltd.; the Executors of the late Mr. Seton Merriman for an extract from *Barlasch of the Guard*, published by Mr. John Murray; Mr. John Murray for material from *Beau Geste* by P. C. Wren; Mr. Lloyd Osbourne for " The Siege of the Round House," from *Kidnapped* by R. L. Stevenson; the Executors of the late Mr. Stanley Weyman for two chapters from *The Red Cockade*.

A BONNY FIGHTER

THIS story is told by David Balfour. At the instigation of his uncle Ebenezer he is kidnapped by Captain Hoseason of the brig *Covenant*. The ship is bound for the Carolinas where David is to be sold as a slave. In a thick fog in the Minch the brig runs down a boat and only one man is saved. This is Alan Breck Stewart, a Jacobite, who is in Scotland to collect rents for his exiled master. Alan bargains with the captain to land him, if possible, in Linnhe Loch, but the sight of the gold in Alan's belt excites the cupidity of captain and crew and they plot to kill him. David, however, warns Alan and the two prepare to defend themselves in the round-house.

A BONNY FIGHTER

BUT now our time of truce was come to an end. Those on deck had waited for my coming till they grew impatient; and scarce had Alan spoken when the captain showed face in the open door.

"Stand!" cried Alan, and pointed his sword at him.

The captain stood, indeed; but he neither winced nor drew back a foot.

"A naked sword?" says he. "This is a strange return for hospitality."

"Do you see me?" said Alan. "I am come of kings; I bear a king's name. My badge is the oak. Do ye see my sword? It has slashed the heads off mair Whigamores than you have toes upon your feet. Call up your vermin to your back, sir, and fall on! The sooner the clash begins, the sooner ye'll taste this steel throughout your vitals."

The captain said nothing to Alan, but he looked over at me with an ugly look. "David," said he, "I'll mind this;" and the sound of his voice went through me with a jar.

Next moment he was gone.

"And now," said Alan, "let your hand keep your head, for the grip is coming."

Alan drew a dirk, which he held in his left hand in case they should run in under his sword. I, on my part, clambered up into the berth with an armful of pistols and something of a heavy heart, and set open the window where I was to watch. It was a small part of the deck that I could overlook, but enough for our purpose. The sea had gone down, and the wind was steady and kept the sails quiet; so that there was a great stillness in the ship, in which I made sure I heard the sound of muttering voices. A little after, and there came a clash of steel upon the deck, by which I knew they were dealing out the cutlasses and one had been let fall: and after that, silence again.

I do not know if I was what you call afraid; but my heart beat like a bird's, both quick and little; and there was a dimness came before my eyes which I continually rubbed away, and which continually returned. As for hope, I had none; but only a darkness of despair and a sort of anger against all the world that made me long to sell my life as dear as I was able. I tried to pray, I remember, but that same hurry of my mind, like a man running, would not suffer me to think upon the words; and my chief wish was to have the thing begin and be done with it.

It came all of a sudden when it did, with a rush of

feet and a roar, and then a shout from Alan, and a sound of blows and someone crying out as if hurt. I looked back over my shoulder, and saw Mr. Shuan in the doorway, crossing blades with Alan.

"That's him that killed the boy! " I cried.

"Look to your window! " said Alan; and as I turned back to my place, I saw him pass his sword through the mate's body.

It was none too soon for me to look to my own part; for my head was scarce back at the window, before five men, carrying a spare yard for a battering-ram, ran past me and took post to drive the door in. I had never fired with a pistol in my life, and not often with a gun; far less against a fellow-creature. But it was now or never; and just as they swang the yard, I cried out, "Take that! " and shot into their midst.

I must have hit one of them, for he sang out and gave back a step, and the rest stopped as if a little disconcerted. Before they had time to recover, I sent another ball over their heads, and at my third shot (which went as wide as the second) the whole party threw down the yard and ran for it.

Then I looked round again into the deck-house. The whole place was full of smoke of my own firing, just as my ears seemed to be burst with the noise of the shots. But there was Alan, standing as before; only now his sword was running blood to the hilt, and himself so swelled with triumph and fallen into so fine an attitude, that he looked to be invincible. Right before him on the floor was Mr. Shuan, on his hands and knees; the blood was pouring from his mouth, and he was sinking slowly lower, with a terrible white face;

and just as I looked, some of those from behind caught hold of him by the heels and dragged him bodily out of the round-house. I believe he died as they were doing it.

"There's one of your Whigs for ye!" cried Alan; and then turning to me, he asked if I had done much execution.

I told him I had winged one, and thought it was the captain.

"And I've settled two," says he. "No, there's not enough blood let; they'll be back again. To your watch, David. This is but a dram before meat."

I settled back to my place, recharging the three pistols I had fired, and keeping watch with both eye and ear.

Our enemies were disputing not far off upon the deck, and that so loudly that I could hear a word or two above the washing of the seas.

"It was Shuan bauchled[1] it," I heard one say.

And another answered him with a "Wheesht, man! He's paid the piper."

After that the voices fell again into the same muttering as before. Only now, one person spoke most of the time, as though laying down a plan, and first one and then another answered him briefly, like men taking orders. By this, I made sure they were coming on again, and told Alan.

"It's what we have to pray for," said he. "Unless we can give them a good distaste of us, and done with it, there'll be nae sleep for either you or me. But this time, mind, they'll be in earnest."

[1] Bungled.

By this, my pistols were ready, and there was nothing to do but listen and wait. While the brush lasted I had not the time to think if I was frightened; but now, when all was still again, my mind ran upon nothing else. The thought of the sharp swords and the cold steel was strong in me; and presently, when I began to hear stealthy steps and a brushing of men's clothes against the round-house wall, and knew they were taking their places in the dark, I could have found it in my mind to cry out aloud.

All this was upon Alan's side; and I began to think my share of the fight was at an end, when I heard someone drop softly on the roof above me.

Then there came a single call on the sea-pipe, and that was the signal. A knot of them made one rush of it, cutlass in hand, against the door; and at the same moment, the glass of the skylight was dashed in a thousand pieces, and a man leaped through and landed on the floor. Before he got his feet, I had clapped a pistol to his back, and might have shot him too; only at the touch of him (and him alive) my whole flesh misgave me, and I could no more pull the trigger than I could have flown.

He had dropped his cutlass as he jumped, and when he felt the pistol, whipped straight round and laid hold of me, roaring out an oath; and at that either my courage came again, or I grew so much afraid as came to the same thing; for I gave a shriek and shot him in the midst of the body. He gave the most horrible, ugly groan, and fell to the floor. The foot of a second fellow, whose legs were dangling through the skylight, struck me at the same time upon the head; and at that

I snatched another pistol and shot this one through the thigh, so that he slipped through and tumbled in a lump on his companion's body. There was no talk of missing, any more than there was time to aim; I clapped the muzzle to the very place and fired.

I might have stood and stared at them for long, but I heard Alan shout as if for help, and that brought me to my senses.

He had kept the door so long; but one of the seamen, while he was engaged with others, had run in under his guard and caught him about the body. Alan was dirking him with his left hand, but the fellow clung like a leech. Another had broken in and had his cutlass raised. The door was thronged with their faces. I thought we were lost, and catching up my cutlass, fell on them in flank.

But I had not time to be of help. The wrestler dropped at last; and Alan, leaping back to get his distance, ran upon the others like a bull, roaring as he went. They broke before him like water, turning, and running, and falling one against the other in their haste. The sword in his hand flashed like quicksilver into the huddle of our fleeing enemies; and at every flash there came the scream of a man hurt. I was still thinking we were lost, when lo! they were all gone, and Alan was driving them along the deck as a sheep-dog chases sheep.

Yet he was no sooner out than he was back again, being as cautious as he was brave; and meanwhile the seamen continued running and crying out as if he was still behind them; and we heard them tumble one upon another into the forecastle, and clap-to the hatch upon the top.

The round-house was like a shambles; three were dead inside, another lay in his death agony across the threshold; and there were Alan and I victorious and unhurt.

He came up to me with open arms. "Come to my arms!" he cried, and embraced and kissed me hard upon both cheeks. "David," said he, "I love you like a brother. And O, man," he cried in a kind of ecstasy, "am I no a bonny fighter?"

Thereupon he turned to the four enemies, passed his sword clean through each of them, and tumbled them out of doors one after the other. As he did so, he kept humming, and singing, and whistling to himself, like a man trying to recall an air; only what *he* was trying was to make one. All the while, the flush was in his face, and his eyes were as bright as a five-year-old child's with a new toy. And presently he sat down upon the table, sword in hand; the air that he was making all the time began to run a little clearer, and then clearer still; and then out he burst with a great voice into a Gaelic song.

I have translated it here, not in verse (of which I have no skill) but at least in the king's English. He sang it often afterwards, and the thing became popular; so that I have heard it, and had it explained to me, many's the time.

> This is the song of the sword of Alan;
> The smith made it,
> The fire set it;
> Now it shines in the hand of Alan Breck.

Their eyes were many and bright,
Swift were they to behold,
Many the hands they guided;
The sword was alone.

The dun deer troop over the hill,
They are many, the hill is one;
The dun deer vanish,
The hill remains.

Come to me from the hills of heather,
Come from the isles of the sea.
O far-beholding eagles,
Here is your meat.

Now this song which he made (both words and music) in the hour of our victory, is something less than just to me, who stood beside him in the tussle. Mr. Shuan and five more were either killed outright or thoroughly disabled; but of these, two fell by my hand, the two that came by the skylight. Four more were hurt, and of that number, one (and he not the least important) got his hurt from me. So that, altogether, I did my fair share both of the killing, and the wounding, and might have claimed a place in Alan's verses. But poets have to think upon their rhymes; and in good prose talk, Alan always did me more than justice.

In the meanwhile, I was innocent of any wrong being done me. For not only I knew no word of the Gaelic; but what with the long suspense of the waiting, and the scurry and strain of our two spirts of fighting, and more than all, the horror I had of some of my own

21

share in it, the thing was no sooner over than I was glad to stagger to a seat. There was that tightness on my chest that I could hardly breathe; the thought of the two men I had shot sat upon me like a nightmare; and all upon a sudden, and before I had a guess of what was following, I began to sob and cry like any child.

Alan clapped my shoulder, and said I was a brave lad and wanted nothing but sleep.

"I'll take the first watch," said he. "You've done well by me, David, first and last; and I wouldn't lose you for all Appin—no, nor for Breadalbane."

So I made up my bed on the floor; and he took the first spell, pistol in hand and sword on knee, three hours by the captain's watch upon the wall. Then he roused me up, and I took my turn of three hours; before the end of which it was broad day, and a very quiet morning, with a smooth, rolling sea that tossed the ship and made the blood run to and fro on the round-house floor, and a heavy rain that drummed upon the roof. All my watch there was nothing stirring; and by the banging of the helm, I knew they had even no one at the tiller. Indeed (as I learned afterwards) there were so many of them hurt or dead, and the rest in so ill a temper, that Mr. Riach and the captain had to take turn and turn like Alan and me, or the brig might have gone ashore and nobody the wiser. It was a mercy the night had fallen so still, for the wind had gone down as soon as the rain began. Even as it was, I judged by the wailing of a great number of gulls that went crying and fishing round the ship, that she must have drifted pretty near the coast or one of the islands of the Hebrides; and at last, looking out of the door of the round-house, I saw the great stone hills of Skye on the right hand, and, a little more astern, the strange isle of Rum.

R. L. STEVENSON—*Kidnapped.*

A HAZARDOUS JOURNEY

THIS is a story of France in the early seventeenth century in the reign of Louis XIII. The Queen, Anne of Austria, has given a set of diamond studs, a gift from the King, to the English Duke of Buckingham. In order to defeat the intrigues of Cardinal Richelieu, the King's adviser, it is necessary for the Queen to have them returned to her. D'Artagnan and his friends, Athos, Porthos, and Aramis, the three musketeers, undertake to go to England on the Queen's behalf. Planchet, Mousqueton, Grimaud, and Bazin are their servants.

A HAZARDOUS JOURNEY

At two o'clock in the morning our four adventurers left Paris, by the Porte St. Denis. Whilst the darkness lasted they continued silent. In spite of themselves, they felt the influence of the obscurity, and suspected an ambuscade at every step.

With the first streak of day, their tongues became unbound, and gaiety returned with the sun. It was as on the eve of battle: the heart beat, and the eyes sparkled; and they felt that the life which they were perhaps, about to leave, was, after all, a pleasant and a precious thing.

The appearance of the cavalcade was of the most formidable character: the black horses of the musketeers, their martial bearing, and that military custom which made these noble chargers march in rank, were all indications of their calling, which would have betrayed the strictest incognito.

The valets followed, armed to the teeth.

All went on well as far as Chantilly, where they arrived at about eight in the morning, and where they were obliged to breakfast. They dismounted at a tavern, which was recommended by the sign of St. Martin, giving half his cloak to a beggar. They ordered their servants not to unsaddle their horses, and to be ready to depart at a moment's notice.

They entered the common room of the inn, and placed themselves at table. A gentleman, who had arrived by the Dampmartin road, was seated at the table, breakfasting. He entered into conversation, concerning the rain and the fine weather. The travellers replied: he drank to their healths, and they returned his politeness. But at the moment when Mousqueton came to announce that the horses were ready, and as they arose from table, the stranger proposed to Porthos, to drink the cardinal's health. Porthos replied, that he desired nothing better, provided the stranger would, in return, drink the health of the king. The stranger exclaimed, that he knew no other king than his eminence. On this, Porthos told him he must be drunk, and the stranger drew his sword.

"You have done a foolish thing," said Athos; "but never mind; you cannot draw back now: kill the fellow, and come after us as fast as you can."

And all three mounted their horses and departed at full speed; while Porthos promised his adversary to perforate him in all the fashions known to the fencing school.

"There goes one of us," said Athos, after they had travelled five hundred paces.

"But why did that man attack Porthos, rather than the others?" said Aramis.

"Because, from Porthos speaking louder than the rest of us, he took him for the leader of the party," said d'Artagnan.

"I always said," muttered Athos, "that the Gascon youth was a well of wisdom."

The travellers proceeded on their way.

At Beauvais they stopped two hours, as much to breathe their horses, as to wait for Porthos. At the end of that time, as neither Porthos nor any intelligence of him had arrived, they resumed their journey.

About a league from Beauvais, at a point where the way was narrowed between two banks, they met eight or ten men, who, taking advantage of the road being unpaved at this place, seemed to be engaged in digging holes, and making muddy ruts.

Aramis, fearing to dirty his boots in this artificial slough, apostrophized them rudely. Athos wished to restrain him, but it was too late. The workmen began to rail at the travellers; and, by their insolence, even ruffled the temper of the cool Athos, who urged his horse against one of them.

At this aggression, each of these men drew back to the ditch, and took from it a musket that was concealed there. The result was, that our seven travellers were literally riddled by shot. Aramis received a ball through the shoulder, and Mousqueton another in the fleshy part of the back, below the loins. But Mousqueton alone fell from his horse; not that he was seriously wounded, but that he could not see his wound, he no doubt thought it far more dangerous than it really was.

"This is an ambuscade," said d'Artagnan: "let us not burn priming, but away."

Aramis, wounded as he was, seized the mane of his horse, which carried him off with the others. That of Mousqueton had rejoined them, and galloped riderless by their side.

"That will give us a spare horse," said Athos.

"I should much prefer a hat," said d'Artagnan, "for mine has been carried off by a ball. It is very lucky, faith, that my letter was not within it."

"Ah! but they will kill poor Porthos, when he comes up," said Aramis.

"If Porthos were upon his legs, he would have rejoined us ere this," said Athos. "It is my opinion, that, in the combat, the drunkard grew sober."

They galloped on for two more hours, although the horses were so fatigued, that it was to be feared they would break down on the way.

The travellers had made a detour by cross-roads, hoping thereby to be less molested; but, at Crevecœur, Aramis declared that he could go no farther. In fact, it had required all the courage which he concealed beneath his elegant form and polished manners, to proceed so far. At each movement he grew paler; and they were at last obliged to support him on his horse. Putting him down at the door of a wine-shop, and leaving with him Bazin, who was more hindrance than help in a skirmish, they set off again, in hopes of reaching Amiens, and passing the night there.

"Zounds!" said Athos, when they found themselves

once more upon the way, reduced to two masters, with Grimaud and Planchet, " Zounds! I will be their dupe no more. I promise you that they shall not make me open my mouth, or draw my sword, between here and Calais. I swear——"

" Don't swear," said d'Artagnan, " but gallop; that is, if our horses will consent to it."

And the travellers dug their spurs into the flanks of their horses, which, thus urged, recovered some degree of strength. They reached Amiens at midnight, and dismounted at the sign of the Golden Lily.

The innkeeper had the look of the most honest fellow upon earth. He received the travellers with a candlestick in one hand, and his cotton nightcap in the other. He wished to lodge the two travellers, each in a charming chamber; but, unfortunately, these two chambers were at opposite extremities of the hotel. D'Artagnan and Athos declined them. The host objected, that he had no others worthy of their excellencies; but they declared that they would rather sleep in the common room, on mattresses, upon the floor. The host insisted, but the travellers were obstinate, and carried their point.

They had just arranged their beds, and barricaded the door, when someone knocked at the shutters. They inquired who was there, and, on recognizing the voices of their servants, opened the window. It was indeed Planchet and Grimaud.

" Grimaud will be quite able to guard the horses," said Planchet, " and if the gentlemen like, I will sleep across their door, by which means they will be certain that no one can get at them."

" And on what will you sleep? " asked d'Artagnan.

" This is my bed," replied Planchet, strewing a bundle of straw.

" Come, then," said d'Artagnan, " you are quite right: the countenance of our host does not at all please me; it is far too polite."

" Nor me, either," said Athos.

Planchet got in at the window, and laid himself across the doorway; whilst Grimaud shut himself up in the stable, promising that at five in the morning he and the four horses should be ready.

The night passed quickly enough. Someone attempted, about two o'clock, to open the door; but, as Planchet awoke with a start, and cried out, " Who is there? " he was answered that it was a mistake; and then the footsteps retreated.

At four in the morning a great noise was heard from the stables. Grimaud had endeavoured to awake the ostlers, and they had made an attack upon him. When the window was opened, they saw the poor fellow lying senseless, with his head split open by a blow from a broom handle.

Planchet went into the courtyard, and wanted to saddle the horses, but the horses were completely foundered. That of Grimaud, which had travelled for five or six hours with an empty saddle the evening before, might have continued its journey; but, by an inconceivable mistake, the veterinary surgeon, whom they had brought, as it appeared, to bleed the landlord's horse, had bled that of Grimaud instead.

This began to be vexatious. All these successive accidents were perhaps the result of chance; but they might also be the effect of design. Athos and d'Artagnan stepped out, whilst Planchet went in to inquire whether there were three horses to be sold in the neighbourhood. At the door were two horses ready saddled, fresh, and vigorous. This was just the thing. He asked where their masters were; and was informed that they had passed the night there, and were now paying their bill.

Athos went down to settle their account, whilst d'Artagnan and Planchet remained at the door. The innkeeper was in a distant lower room, which Athos was requested to enter.

Athos went in confidently, and took out two pistoles to pay. The host was alone, and seated at his desk, one of the drawers of which was partly open. He took the money which Athos gave him, turned it over in his hands, and suddenly exclaiming that the pieces were bad, declared that he would have him and his companion arrested as passers of false coin.

"You rascal," said Athos, as he went towards him, "I will cut off your ears."

But the host stooped down, and taking two pistols from the drawer, presented them at Athos, vociferating, at the same time, for help.

At that very moment, four men, armed to the teeth, rushed in through the side door, and fell upon Athos.

"I am seized!" bawled Athos, with the utmost strength of his lungs; "away with you, d'Artagnan; spur on! spur on!" and he fired off his two pistols.

D'Artagnan and Planchet did not wait to be twice warned. They unfastened the two horses which were standing at the door, jumped upon them, dug the spurs into their flanks, and went off at full gallop.

"Do you know what has become of Athos?" asked d'Artagnan, as they hurried on.

"Oh, sir," said Planchet, "I saw two men fall at his two shots, and it seemed to me, through the window, as if he were working away at the others with his sword."

"Brave Athos!" ejaculated d'Artagnan. "And then to know that I must abandon you! Well! the same thing awaits us, perhaps, at ten paces hence. Forward! Planchet, forward! You are a brave fellow."

"I told you so, sir," replied Planchet; "the Picards are only known by being used. Besides, I am in my own country here, and that stimulates me."

And both of them, spurring on as fast as possible, arrived at St. Omer without a moment's stay. At St. Omer they breathed their horses, with their bridles looped on their arms for fear of accidents, and ate a morsel standing in the street; after which they again set off.

At a hundred paces from the gate of Calais, d'Artagnan's horse fell, and could by no means be got up again; the blood gushed from his eyes and nose. That of Planchet still remained; but he had chosen to halt, and nothing could induce him to continue his exertions.

Fortunately, as we have said, they were only a hundred paces from the town. They therefore left the two steeds upon the high road, and ran to the harbour. Planchet made his master remark a gentleman who had just arrived with his lackey, and was not above fifty yards before them.

They hastily drew near this gentleman, who appeared

to be exceedingly busy. His boots were covered with dust, and he inquired whether he could not pass over to England instantly.

"Nothing easier," replied the master of a vessel then ready for sailing, "but an order arrived this morning to let no one leave without permission from the cardinal."

"I have got that permission," said the gentleman, drawing a paper from his pocket; "there it is."

"Get it countersigned by the governor of the port," said the master of the vessel, "and give me the preference."

"Where shall I find the governor?"

"At his country house."

"And where is his country house situated?"

"At a quarter of a league from the town: see, you may distinguish it from here—yonder slated roof, at the foot of the little hill."

"Very well," said the gentleman; and, followed by his servant, he took the road to the governor's country house.

D'Artagnan and Planchet followed him, at the distance of five hundred yards.

Once out of the town, d'Artagnan hurried forward, and made up on the gentleman as he entered a small wood.

"Sir," said d'Artagnan, "you appear in particular haste?"

"No one can be more so, sir."

"I am very sorry for it," said d'Artagnan, "for, as I am in a hurry also, I want you to render me a favour."

"What is it?"

"To let me pass the Straits before you."

"Impossible!" said the gentleman. "I have done sixty leagues in forty-four hours, and I must be in London by noon to-morrow."

"And I," said d'Artagnan, "have gone the same distance in forty hours, and must be in London by ten o'clock to-morrow."

"Sorry to disappoint you, sir; but I have got here first, and will not go over second."

"I am grieved also, sir," said d'Artagnan, "but I have got here second, and mean to go over first."

"The king's service!" said the gentleman.

"My own service!" replied d'Artagnan.

"But, it seems to me, that this is a poor quarrel which you are seeking to make?"

"Zounds! what would you have it?"

"What do you want?"

"Do you want to know?"

"Certainly."

"Very well! I want the order that you have in your pocket, as I have none, and you must have one."

"I presume you are joking."

"I never joke!"

"Let me pass, sir."

"You shall not pass."

"My gallant, I will blow your brains out. Hollo! Lubin, my pistols."

"Planchet," said d'Artagnan, "take care of the man —I will manage the master."

Planchet, encouraged by what had already happened, rushed upon Lubin, and as he was strong and vigorous, laid him on his back, and put his knees upon his breast.

" Do your business, sir," said Planchet to his master, " I have settled mine."

Seeing this, the gentleman drew his sword, and fell on d'Artagnan; but he had to do with rather a tough customer.

In three seconds d'Artagnan gave him three wounds, saying, at each thrust—

" One for Athos, one for Porthos, and one for Aramis."

At the third stroke the gentleman fell like a log.

D'Artagnan thought he was dead, or at least that he had fainted, and approached him to seize the order; but, at the moment that he stretched out his hand to search for it, the wounded man, who had not dropped his sword, stabbed him with it on the chest, saying—

" One for you! "

" And one more for you! and the best last! " cried d'Artagnan, furiously pinning him to the earth with a fourth wound through the body.

This time the gentleman closed his eyes and fainted.

D'Artagnan felt in the pocket where he had seen him place the order for his passage, and took it. It was in the name of the Count de Wardes.

Then, throwing a last glance on the handsome young man, who was scarcely twenty-five years old, and whom he left lying there senseless, and perhaps dead, he breathed a sigh at the strange destiny which leads men to destroy each other for the interests of those they scarcely know, and who often are not even aware of their existence.

But he was soon disturbed in these reflections by

Lubin, who was howling with all his might, and crying for aid.

Planchet put his hand upon his throat, and squeezed it as hard as he could.

" Sir," said he, " as long as I hold him so, he will not cry out; but the moment I leave go, he will begin again. I can see he is a Norman, and the Normans are monstrously obstinate."

In fact, squeezed as he was, Lubin still endeavoured to sound his pipes.

" Stop! " said d'Artagnan; and, taking his handkerchief, he gagged him.

" Now," said Planchet, " let us bind him to a tree."

The thing was properly done. They then placed the Count de Wardes near his servant; and, as the night began to fall, and as both the bound man and the wounded one were some paces in the wood, it was clear that they must remain there till the next morning.

" And now," said d'Artagnan, " to the house of the governor."

" You are wounded, I fear? " said Planchet.

" It is nothing: let us now think of what is of the most consequence; we can attend to my wound afterwards; besides, it does not appear to be very dangerous."

And they both proceeded, with prodigious strides, towards the country house of the worthy functionary.

The Count de Wardes was announced.

D'Artagnan was introduced.

" Have you an order signed by the cardinal? " asked the governor.

" Yes, sir," said d'Artagnan, " here it is."

"Ah! Ah! it is regular and explicit," said the governor.

"That is quite natural," answered d'Artagnan; "I am one of his most faithful servants."

"It appears that his eminence wishes to hinder some-one from reaching England."

"Yes, a certain d'Artagnan, a Bearnese gentleman, who left Paris with three of his friends, intending to go to London."

"Do you know him personally?" inquired the governor.

"Whom?"

"This d'Artagnan."

"Perfectly well."

"Give me some description of him, then."

"Nothing is easier."

And then d'Artagnan gave, feature for feature, the exact description of the Count de Wardes.

"Has he any attendant?" demanded the governor.

"Yes, a servant named Lubin."

"We will watch for them, and, if we can lay hands upon them, his eminence may be assured that they shall be sent back to Paris under a sufficient escort."

"In so doing, sir," said d'Artagnan, "you will merit the gratitude of the cardinal."

"Will you see him on your return, count?"

"Without doubt."

"Tell him, I beseech you," said the governor, "that I am his most humble servant."

"I will not fail to do so."

Delighted by this assurance, the governor counter-signed the order, and returned it to d'Artagnan; who lost no time in useless compliments, but, having bowed to him and thanked him, took his leave.

Once out of the house, they took a circuitous path to avoid the wood, and entered the town by another gate.

The barque was still ready to sail, and the master waited on the quay.

" Well? " said he, seeing d'Artagnan.

" Here is my pass countersigned."

" And the other gentleman."

" He is not going over to-day," said d'Artagnan; " but make yourself easy, I will pay for the passage of both."

" In that case, let us be off," said the master.

" Away, then! " cried d'Artagnan; and he and Planchet springing into the boat, in five minutes they were on board the vessel.

It was full time, for when they were a half league out at sea, d'Artagnan saw a flash, and heard a detonation; it was the sound of the cannon that announced the closing of the port.

It was now time to think about his wound. Happily it was, as d'Artagnan had supposed, not at all dangerous; the point of the sword had stuck against a rib, and glanced along the bone; and, as the shirt had stuck to the wound at once, scarcely a drop of blood had flowed.

D'Artagnan was overpowered with fatigue; and a mattress being spread for him on the deck, he threw himself upon it and slept.

The next morning, at break of day, he found himself at not less than three or four leagues from the shores of England. The wind had been gentle during the night, and they had made but little progress.

At two o'clock they cast anchor in the harbour of

Dover, and at half-past two d'Artagnan landed in England, exclaiming:

"Here I am, at last."

But this was not enough; he must get to London. In England posting was pretty well regulated. D'Artagnan and Planchet took each a post-horse; a postillion galloped before them; and in a few hours they reached the gates of London.

The duke was hunting, at Windsor, with the king.

D'Artagnan knew nothing of London; he knew not one word of English; but he wrote the word *Buckingham* on a piece of paper, and everyone could direct him to the mansion of the duke.

D'Artagnan inquired for the duke's confidential valet, who, having accompanied him in all his journeys, spoke French perfectly. He told him that he came from Paris on an affair of life and death, and that he must speak with his master without an instant's delay.

The confidence with which d'Artagnan spoke satisfied Patrick (for that was the name of the minister's minister). He ordered two horses to be saddled, and took upon himself the charge of guiding the young guardsman. As for poor Planchet, they had taken him off his horse as stiff as a stake. The poor fellow was quite exhausted; but d'Artagnan seemed to be made of iron.

They reached Windsor Castle, where they learned that the king and the duke were out hawking, in some marshes, two or three miles off.

In twenty minutes they reached the place. Patrick heard his master's voice, calling his hawk.

" Whom shall I announce to my lord? " said Patrick.

"The young man," said d'Artagnan, "who sought a quarrel with him one evening on the Pont Neuf, opposite the Samaritan."

"A strange recommendation," said Patrick.

"You will see that it is as good as any one could be."

Patrick gave his horse the rein, reached the duke, and told him, in the very words which we have just used, that a messenger awaited him.

Buckingham at once remembered d'Artagnan; and fearing that something had happened in France, of which information had been sent to him, he only gave himself time to ask where the messenger was; and having recognized the uniform of the guards at that distance, he rode at full speed straight up to d'Artagnan. Patrick judiciously kept himself in the background.

"No misfortune has befallen the queen?" cried Buckingham.

"I think not, sir; but I believe that she is in great danger, from which your grace alone can rescue her."

"I," said Buckingham; "and how shall I be sufficiently happy to render her any service? Speak! speak!"

"Take this letter," said d'Artagnan.

"This letter! and from whom comes this letter?"

"From her majesty, I believe."

"From her majesty," said Buckingham, growing so pale that d'Artagnan thought he was about to fall.

And he broke the seal.

"What is this rent?" asked he, showing d'Artagnan a place where it was pierced through.

"Ah!" said d'Artagnan, "I did not perceive it before: the sword of the Count de Wardes must have done that, when it was boring a hole in my chest."

"Are you wounded?" inquired Buckingham.

"Oh! a mere trifle," said d'Artagnan—"a mere scratch."

"Just Heaven! what have I read?" exclaimed Buckingham. "Patrick, remain here—or, rather, find the king, wherever he may be, and tell his majesty that I humbly beseech him to excuse me, but that an affair of the very greatest importance calls me to London. Come, sir, come."

And both took their way to the capital at full gallop.

ALEXANDRE DUMAS—*The Three Musketeers.*

B*

DOWN GOLDEN FALLS

ERIC BRIGHTEYES, a young yeoman, son of Thorgrimur Iron-toe, is in love with Gudruda, daughter of Asmund Asmund-son, the wisest and wealthiest man in the south of Iceland. Swanhild, daughter of Groa and half-sister of Gudruda, is in love with Eric and she and her mother plot against the happiness of the lovers. They so influence Asmund that he forbids Eric to come to his Yule-tide feast unless he comes down Golden Falls. Ospakar Blacktooth is a mighty warrior from the north of Iceland who has come to Middalhof to seek Gudruda in marriage.

DOWN GOLDEN FALLS

ON this same day Eric rode up from his farm on Ran River and took his road along the brow of Coldback till he came to Stonefell. Now all along Coldback and Stonefell is a steep cliff facing to the south, that grows ever higher till it comes to that point where Golden River falls over it, and, parting its waters below, runs east and west—the branch to the east being called Ran River and that to the west Laxà—for these two streams girdle round the rich plain of Middalhof, till at length they reach the sea. But in the midst of Golden River, on the edge of the cliff, a mass of rock juts up, called Sheep-saddle, dividing the waters of the fall, and over this the spray flies, and in winter the ice gathers, but the river does not cover it. The great fall is thirty fathoms deep, and shaped like a horseshoe, of which the points lie towards Middalhof. Yet if he could but gain the Sheep-saddle rock that divides the midst of the waters, a strong and hardy man might climb down some fifteen fathoms of this depth and scarcely wet his feet.

Now here at the foot of Sheep-saddle rock the double arches of waters meet, and fall in one torrent into the bottomless pool below. But, some three fathoms from this point of the meeting waters, and beneath it, just where the curve is deepest, a single crag, as large as a drinking table and no larger, juts through the foam, and, if a man could reach it, he might leap from it some twelve fathoms, sheer into the spray-hidden pit beneath, there to sink or swim as it might befall. This crag is called Wolf's Fang.

Now Eric stood for a long while on the edge of the fall and looked, measuring everything with his eye. Then he went up above, where the river swirls down to the precipice, and looked again, for it is from this bank that the dividing island-rock Sheep-saddle must be reached.

"A man may hardly do this thing; yet I will try it," he said to himself at last. "My honour shall be great for the feat, if I chance to live, and if I die—well, there is an end of troubling after maids and all other things."

So he went home and sat silent that evening. Now, since Thorgrimur Iron-toe's death, his housewife, Saevuna, Eric's mother, had grown dim of sight, and, though she peered and peered again from her seat in the ingle nook, she could not see the face of her son.

"What ails thee, Eric, that thou sittest so silent? Was not the meat, then, to thy mind at supper?"

"Yes, mother, the meat was well enough, though a little undersmoked."

"Now I see that thou art not thyself, son, for thou hadst no meat, but only stock-fish—and I never knew a man forget his supper on the night of its eating, except he was distraught or deep in love."

"Was it so?" said Brighteyes.

"What troubles thee, Eric?—that sweet lass yonder?"

"Ay, somewhat, mother."

"What more, then?"

"This, that I go down Golden Falls to-morrow, and I do not know how I may come from Sheep-saddle rock to Wolf's Fang crag and keep my life whole in me; and now, I pray thee, weary me not with words, for my brain is slow, and I must use it."

When she heard this Saevuna screamed aloud, and threw herself before Eric, praying him to forgo his mad venture. But he would not listen to her, for he was slow to make up his mind, but, that being made up, nothing could change it. Then, when she learned that it was to get sight of Gudruda that he purposed thus to throw his life away, she was very angry and cursed her and all her kith and kin.

"It is likely enough that thou wilt have cause to use such words before all this tale is told," said Eric; "nevertheless, mother, forbear to curse Gudruda, who is in no way to blame for these matters."

"Thou art a faithless son," Saevuna said, "who wilt slay thyself striving to win speech with thy May, and leave thy mother childless."

Eric said that it seemed so indeed, but he was plighted to it and the feat must be tried. Then he kissed her, and she sought her bed weeping.

45

Now it was the day of the Yule-feast, and there was no sun till one hour before noon. But Eric, having kissed his mother and bidden her farewell, called a thrall, Jon by name, and, giving him a sealskin bag full of his best apparel, bade him ride to Middalhof and tell Asmund the Priest that Eric Brighteyes would come down Golden Falls an hour after midday to join his feast; and thence go to the foot of the Golden Falls, to await him there. And the man went, wondering, for he thought his master mad.

Then Eric took a good rope and a staff tipped with iron, and, so soon as the light served, mounted his horse, forded Ran River, and rode along Coldback till he came to the lip of Golden Falls. Here he stayed a while till at length he saw many people streaming up the snow from Middalhof far beneath, and, among them, two women who by their stature should be Gud-ruda and Swanhild, and, near to them, a great man whom he did not know. Then he showed himself for a space on the brink of the gulf and turned his horse upstream. The sun shone bright upon the edge of the sky, but the frost bit like a sword. Still, he must strip off his garments, so that nothing remained on him except his sheepskin shoes, shirt, and hose, and take the water. Now here the river runs mightily, and he must cross full thirty fathoms of the swirling water before he can reach Sheep-saddle, and woe to him if his foot should slip on the boulders, for then certainly he must be swept over the brink.

Eric rested the staff against the stony bottom and, leaning his weight on it, took the stream, and he was so strong that it could not prevail against him till at

46

length he was rather more than half-way across and the water swept above his shoulders. Now he was lifted from his feet, and, letting the staff float, he swam for his life, and with such mighty strokes that he felt little of that icy cold. Down he was swept—now the lip of the fall was but three fathoms away on his left, and already the green water boiled beneath him. A fathom from him was the corner of Sheep-saddle. If he may grasp it, all is well; if not, he dies.

Three great strokes and he held it. His feet were swept out over the brink of the fall, but he clung on grimly, and by the strength of his arms drew himself on to the rock and rested a while. Presently he stood up, for the cold began to nip him, and the people below became aware that he had swum the river above the fall and raised a shout, for the deed was great. Now Eric must begin to clamber down Sheep-saddle, and this was no easy task, for the rock is almost sheer, and slippery with ice, and on either side the waters rushed and thundered, throwing their blinding spray about him as they leapt to the depths beneath. He looked, studying the rock; then, feeling that he grew afraid, made an end of doubt and, grasping a point with both hands, swung himself down his own length and more. Now for many minutes he climbed down Sheep-saddle, and the task was hard, for he was bewildered with the booming of the waters that bent out on either side of him like the arc of a bow, and the rock was very steep and slippery. Still, he came down all those fifteen fathoms and fell not, though twice he was near to falling, and the watchers below marvelled greatly at his hardihood.

"He will be dashed to pieces where the waters meet," said Ospakar, "he can never gain Wolf's Fang crag beneath; and, if so be it that he come there and leaps to the pool, the weight of water will drive him down and drown him."

"It is certainly so," quoth Asmund, "and it grieves me much; for it was my jest that drove him to this perilous adventure, and we cannot spare such a man as Eric Brighteyes."

Now Swanhild turned white as death; but Gudruda said: "If great heart and strength and skill may avail at all, then Eric shall come safely down the waters."

"Thou fool!" whispered Swanhild in her ear, "how can these help him? No troll could live in yonder cauldron. Dead is Eric, and thou art the bait that lured him to his death!"

"Spare thy words," she answered; "as the Norns have ordered so it shall be."

Now Eric stood at the foot of Sheep-saddle, and within an arm's length the mighty waters met, tossing their yellow waves and seething furiously as they leapt to the mist-hid gulf beneath. He bent over and looked through the spray. Three fathoms under him the rock Wolf's Fang split the waters, and thence, if he can come thither, he may leap sheer into the pool below. Now he unwound the rope that was about his middle, and made one end fast to a knob of rock—and this was difficult, for his hands were stiff with cold—and the other end he passed through his leathern girdle. Then Eric looked again, and his heart sank within him. How might he give himself to this boiling flood and not be shattered? But as he looked, lo! a rainbow grew upon the face of the water, and one end of it lit upon him, and the other, like a glory from the Gods, fell full upon Gudruda as she stood a little way apart, watching at the foot of Golden Falls.

"Seest thou that," said Asmund to Groa, who was at his side, "the Gods build their Bifrost bridge between these two. Who now shall keep them asunder?"

"Read the portent thus," she answered: "they shall be united, but not here. Yon is a Spirit bridge, and, see: the waters of Death foam and fall between them!"

Eric, too, saw the omen and it seemed good to him, and all fear left his heart. Round about him the waters thundered, but amidst their roar he dreamed that he heard a voice calling:

"Be of good cheer, Eric Brighteyes; for thou shalt live to do mightier deeds than this, and in guerdon thou shalt win Gudruda."

So he paused no longer, but, shortening up the rope, pulled on it with all his strength, and then leapt out upon the arch of waters. They struck him and he was dashed out like a stone from a sling; again he fell against them and again was dashed away, so that his girdle burst. Eric felt it go and clung wildly to the rope and lo! with the inward swing, he fell on Wolf's Fang, where never a man has stood before and never a man shall stand again. Eric lay a little while on the rock till his breath came back to him, and he listened to the roar of the waters. Then, rising on his hands and knees, he crept to its point, for he could scarcely stand because of the trembling of the stone beneath the shock of the fall; and when the people below saw that he was not dead, they raised a great shout, and the sound of their voices came to him through the noise of the waters.

Now, twelve fathoms beneath him was the surface of the pool; but he could not see it because of the wreaths of spray. Nevertheless, he must leap and that swiftly, for he grew cold. So of a sudden Eric stood up to his full height, and, with a loud cry and a mighty spring, he bounded out from the point of Wolf's Fang far into the air, beyond the reach of the falling flood, and rushed headlong towards the gulf beneath. Now all men watching held their breath as his body travelled, and so great is the place and so high the leap that through the mist Eric seemed but as a big white stone hurled down the face of the arching waters.

He was gone, and the watchers rushed down to the foot of the pool, for there, if he rose at all, he must pass to the shallows. Swanhild could look no more, but sank upon the ground. The face of Gudruda was set like a stone with doubt and anguish. Ospakar saw and read the meaning, and he said to himself: " Now Odin grant that this youngling rise not again! for the maid loves him dearly, and he is too much a man to be lightly swept aside."

Eric struck the pool. Down he sank, and down and down—for the water falling from so far must almost reach the bottom of the pool before it can rise again— and he with it. Now he touched the bottom, but very gently, and slowly began to rise, and, as he rose, was carried along by the stream. But it was long before he could breathe, and it seemed to him that his lungs would burst. Still, he struggled up, striking great strokes with his legs.

"Farewell to Eric," said Asmund, "he will rise no more now."

But just as he spoke Gudruda pointed to something that gleamed, white and golden, beneath the surface of the current, and lo! the bright hair of Eric rose from the water, and he drew a great breath, shaking his head like a seal, and, though but feebly, struck out for the shallows that are at the foot of the pool. Now he found footing, but was swept over by the fierce current, and cut his forehead, and he carried that scar till his death. Again he rose, and with a rush gained the bank unaided and fell upon the snow.

Now people gathered about him in silence and wondering, for none had known so great a deed. And presently Eric opened his eyes and looked up, and found the eyes of Gudruda fixed on his, and there was that in them which made him glad he had dared the path of Golden Falls.

H. RIDER HAGGARD— *Eric Brighteyes.*

THE FIRST SHOT

THIS is the first of a series of short stories dealing with the adventures of the *Thorgrim* and her crew while whale-hunting in Icelandic waters.

THE FIRST SHOT

THE grey sea swells sluggishly under spiritless ripples, the grey atmosphere is bleak, clammy, disheartening; through a rift in the grey curtain of fog lies a glimmer of grey ice. And a grey living thing, parting the sea's surface, emits with a hissing, snoring noise a lofty spreading jet of grey vapour, glides forward, bulges up-ward, slides downward, and vanishes beneath oily eddies, to reappear presently a hundred yards away.

In the intervals between the long-drawn blasts of the grey living thing are heard but two sounds; the faint, constant groaning of the swell on the distant ice and a muffled, rapid, regular throbbing that is not of nature.

As the throbbing grows plainer a shape is born in the mist, dim, uncertain at first, but soon distinguish-able as a ship. She is a small black steamer, no more than ninety feet in length, with a tall, thin funnel and two masts; she is high bowed, and so deep at the stern that her propeller leaves little foam on the troubled grey. Her foremast carries a narrow white barrel, from which appear a man's shoulders and head, also a hand in a thick woollen fingerless glove, gesticulating, pointing. In her bows is a foot high platform carrying a short swivel cannon painted scarlet. From the muzzle protrudes a weapon pointed with a slim cast-iron shell and furnished with four hinged barbs, now folded against the shaft, four feet of which are within the cannon. Under the muzzle, and overhanging the stem, is a tray bearing about fifty fathoms of four-inch cable, an end of which is fastened to a ring in the slotted shaft of the weapon. And, with his hand on the wooden stock whereby the cannon is manipulated, stands a man whose whole attention is directed upon the sea immediately ahead.

His tanned countenance is almost lost in a grizzled beard; his blue eyes are sunken deep in their wrinkled sockets. A shabby fur cap protects his head, a heavy fur waistcoat with sleeves warms his body; ancient pepper and salt trousers, patched and stained, and sea boots cover his nether limbs. Now and then with his free arm he signals, without turning his head, to the steersman in the box high in front of the funnel, and the steersman alters the course, or mutters into the speaking-tube on his right.

The throbbing slows; it ceases. The steamer slips onward in a cautious, stealthy fashion. Fifty fathoms ahead a shadowy bulk moves leisurely from the depths to the surface. The man aloft cries out and points. The gunner nods; his feet take a grip of the spars on the platform; he bends forward. A few yards behind him a man grasps the lever of one of the two powerful winches. Other men come forward and stand watching the sea ahead.

Now there is no sound save the far-off groaning, for the steamer, her way diminishing, is travelling with the swell and moving noiselessly. But the quietness is short-lived.

Not twenty fathoms away the surface breaks; the head of the grey living thing appears, the grey jet shoots up with its accompanying snore. The head sinks; out and up heave the great shoulders and back. The gunner takes what seems an interminable aim at the streaming flank. . . . At last his forefinger twitches.

An orange flame spurts into the grey; a crash shocks the atmosphere; the little steamer shudders as though she had run against a rock; through the white reek fly wads and whirling coils of hemp; and almost under the bows the sea boils and surges. The grey living thing has gone. A dulled thump comes up from the depths.

There is a rumble, a clank of machinery, as the cable flows from the winch and over the bow wheel. The propeller thuds; the steamer begins to go slowly astern. The gunner steps out from the platform, but keeps an eye on the cable. A couple of seamen come forward to sponge out and reload the gun. The lookout, the steersman, and the winchman remain on the alert.

At the end of that yellow cable, fathoms and fathoms below that sullen grey surface, the most stupendous of things created—leviathan himself—stricken sore, struggles and strains for dear life . . . in vain.

All this happened about four o'clock on a July morning, at a place in the Arctic Ocean a hundred miles north of the north-west promontory of Iceland, and close to the rim of the Greenland ice. There, or thereabouts, the whalers of the Norwegian companies stationed on the northern coast of Iceland were now compelled to cruise in search of the big rorquals which, with each succeeding summer of the past twenty years, had been giving Icelandic waters a wider berth, either because their great bellies could no longer be satisfied in their former haunts, or because their comparatively small brains were becoming less and less vaguely informed with a fear of man and his works.

The sun had risen three hours ago; indeed, it had never wholly set, midnight having witnessed a narrow arc of fire above the horizon; but the ice-fog gathering since then had thickened high and low until it had won the morning for its own. It was a bitter morning even for hard-bitten whalemen, and especially for those of the *Thorgrim's* crew who had been on duty since midnight. At this time of year, given moderate weather, there was no hour in the twenty-four that held an excuse for lying-to; round and round the clock the cruising in search of whales, or the actual hunting, went on.

Old Svendsen, gunner and captain, stamped his feet and flapped his arms violently across his wide chest.

Sigurd the *styrmand* (mate), fresh from the crow's-nest, wiped the cold moisture from his short, tawny beard and accepted the mug of steaming coffee which a man had fetched him from the galley.

"Quick work," he remarked in a congratulatory tone. "It is a long time since I saw such a big *blaahval* (blue-whale) killed so smartly. And he is a mighty big one. See how *Thorgrim* is down at the bow!" For the whale had died without coming once to the surface, and the carcass was now suspended some seventy fathoms below the steamer.

"It was a good shot," the gunner returned in his matter-of-fact way. He yawned and produced his pipe. "We were lucky to come on him so soon after losing that *finhval* [1] in the fog. I think we shall go east again. The *finhval* would not be alone." He looked at his watch. "Get the *blaahval* up and alongside as fast as you can, and call me when it is done." Yawning again, he went heavily aft and descended into the little cabin near the stern.

While he slept the ninety-ton carcass was hoisted, slowly and watchfully, to the surface. On its arrival there the great sinewy flukes were cut from the tail and taken on board, to be sold later to the Icelanders, who would pickle and, in due course, eat them; the abdomen was inflated by air pumped through a hollow lance, the wound being afterwards carefully plugged; and when buoyancy for towing was assured, the prize was made fast to the port bow by a massive chain shackled round and through the shank of the tail. These operations occupied a couple of hours, and by the time the whaler started eastwards the weather was showing a promise of improvement.

At 7.30, when Svendsen and his mate came up from

[1] Fin-whale—the second largest species of rorqual.

breakfast, the sun was asserting his power and the fog was thinning before it. Through the lingering veil the sky showed faintly blue and the ripples were beginning to shimmer. The haze still hung thickly on the ice-field, now several miles away, but here and there a drifting ice-pan caught the light and became a thing of beauty, despite its rottenness.

The old gunner was in the best of humours. "Stay, Sigurd," he said as the young man was about to leave him for another spell in the crow's-nest. He lowered his voice and spoke in confidential fashion. "If I do not kill the next whale with one shot, you can take the second shot."

"*Tak!*" said Sigurd, looking pleased.

"And if we find a third whale to-day, I will give you the first shot!"

At this Sigurd fairly beamed and impulsively grasped his skipper's hand.

"'Sh!" whispered the old man. "We will keep it a secret till the time comes." With a friendly nod he turned away and mounted the iron ladder to the steering-box.

Sigurd took his place in the crow's-nest in an unwonted state of excitement. The whaleman who has the ambition, as Sigurd had, to become a gunner is entirely dependent on the goodwill of his captain for opportunities of practice in shooting. Under some captains patience may become despair. Old Svendsen, however, was generous where youth was concerned. He would not have grudged his lieutenant the most brilliant shot of the *Thorgrim's* long record. He was ready to stake the loss of a valuable whale and his own bounty on its capture, not to mention the approval of his employers and the confidence of his crew, in order that the young man should have his chance. And on this occasion his generosity was greater than the mate could have imagined.

Sigurd had already enjoyed a good many chances during the present season, but not until to-day had his skipper mentioned the possibility of a "first shot." To Sigurd it was an unexpected step—nay, a leap—nearer his goal. Already he imagined himself firing a shot as swiftly fatal as that which he had witnessed a few hours ago. He had a reputation for keen sight, and if he did not now exercise his eyes more conscientiously than in the past, there was surely a new eagerness in his gaze.

The increasing clarity of the atmosphere favoured his search. Save in the direction of the still fog-ridden ice, his sight had an unobstructed range of several miles. The blues of the sky and the widening expanse of ocean deepened. Under a light breeze the ripples became tiny breakers, through which the *Thorgrim* cut crisply, her monstrous flabby captive wallowing and surging alongside. There was warmth in the sunshine, and Sigurd, in his bobbing, quivering refuge, sang cheerfully to himself. At the end of two hours a sailor clambered up to relieve him, but he sent the man back with permission to turn in for an extra spell, if he felt so inclined. Old Svendsen, sunning himself and smoking in a corner of the steering-box, grinned and bawled: " Sigurd! "

" *Ja?* " responded the mate, without taking his gaze from the sea.

59

"Shall I send you up the big glass?" This was an old gibe at Sigurd, who was inclined to be superior regarding optical assistance.

Sigurd returned an ironic *tak* (thanks) and gave a direction to the steersman, who altered the course and at the same time, spoke into the tube: "Full speed."

"*Blaast?*" (Blow?) quickly queried the old man, straightening his back and peering.

Sigurd held up three fingers—then expanded his hand.

"*Finhval?*" asked Svendsen.

"I think so." Thus far Sigurd had descried nothing more than faint puffs of vapour above the distant surface. It is doubtful whether any other man on board would have detected them. From their number he was almost certain that they rose from fin-whales, but until he could better estimate the height of the "spouts" he could not be positive that they were not from the largest rorquals, blue-whales.

Meanwhile there was some stir on the forward deck of the *Thorgrim*. Men were adjusting the heavy chain so that the dead whale might be cast adrift at a moment's notice. Svendsen appeared with a Norwegian ensign bound to the pole of a lance, the point of which he drove deep into the carcass. Afterwards he looked to his gun, oiled the swivel bearings, and inserted the Krupp firing screw.

"*Finhval,*" Sigurd definitely announced. There was a hint of disappointment in his voice, for he had hoped against hope for *blaahval*. The biggest sort of whale could not be big enough for his "first shot." Nevertheless, he admitted himself fortunate in his skipper, and prayed for a seventy-foot *finhval* when his turn came. As for the "second shot" promised by Svendsen, he began to wish that it might not be necessary. True, it might help him to "get his hand in"; at the same time, it would be just as likely, even if it proved an excellent shot, to leave his nerves jumpy for what he felt was going to be the moment of his life. Yet he could hardly refuse to take the "second shot." All he could do was to hope that Svendsen's aim might be as deadly now as in the early morning.

The sighting of a whale is too often but the beginning of a long, dreary chase, but these fin-whales were not on the move just then. They were feeding, and the food, it seemed, was plenteous, for they kept within the space of a square mile. Hence the *Thorgrim*, handicapped as she was with her burden alongside, was not long in coming to close quarters.

Sigurd could distinguish the roof of each head as it broke the surface, and the spurt of vapour as it expanded to a cloudlet that drifted over the face of the waters for an appreciable time ere it was dispersed. The curving back and the prominent fin set far aft were plain to those on deck, while the hoarse expirations came distinctly to their ears.

The *Thorgrim's* engines were stopped, and she was brought to rest while the dead blue-whale was let go. Afterwards she was manœuvred away from the carcass, and with the utmost caution, for not so long ago one of the company's whalers had lost her rudder and two blades of her propeller through an apparently mild collision with her prize. Then, at half speed, she made quietly in the direction of the living whales.

Svendsen signed to Sigurd to descend, and dispatched a man to take his place.

" *Ja,* Kaptein? " said Sigurd as he joined the old man. " What is it you want with me? " It was early enough, he thought, to stand by for the possible " second shot." " Shall I take the wheel now? " he inquired, after waiting in vain for a reply to his questions. Svendsen was staring ahead in absent-minded fashion.

" I have changed my mind, Sigurd," the old man said slowly at last. " I do not wish you to take the second shot."

The mate's face fell, whereas one would have expected it to lighten.

" And if there is a second whale," Svendsen continued, " I do not wish you to take the first shot."

The mate averted a countenance that burned with anger as well as disappointment, and moved away.

" But," said the old man, following and laying a hand on his shoulder, " I give you the first shot *now.* Shoot well! " He spoke a word to the men near by, intimating that the mate was gunner and in charge, and was well on his way to the steering-box before the other was fit to express himself.

Sigurd, looking as self-conscious as a schoolboy coming upon the stage to deliver his first recitation, mounted the platform.

" Good luck," said the winchman, while the others grinned. " What will you give us if you miss him? "

" I will give you the blame, Johan."

" I will bet a *krone* you miss him," said Johan, noticing that Sigurd's hand shook as he turned the key which set the gun free on its bearings.

" Done! "

" Also I will bet you three *kroner* you do not kill him with one harpoon."

" Done! "

" Mind, Sigurd," said the winchman solemnly, " you must try to shoot him between the head and the tail."

There was a general laugh, in which Sigurd joined.

The elderly cook appeared from the galley with a mug of coffee, which he offered to Sigurd, saying, " Make sure your hands are warm. When I was a gunner——"

" When was that, Hansen? " cried Johan, guffawing.

" When you were in petticoats, my pretty boy."

" I do not believe you have ever shot a whale," retorted the winchman, who was rather sensitive about his ugly countenance.

" I was talking of rabbits, which I never miss when my hands are warm," the cook replied, with grave dignity. " Now, I will bet you, Johan, five *kroner* that Sigurd takes his whale with one shot."

" And if you lose we shall all get bad grub for a fortnight. *Nei, tak!* "

After that there was silence. They were among the whales, and not even Johan desired to see the mate fail.

The *Thorgrim* began to stalk a couple that seemed to have gorged themselves, for they swam at a most leisurely pace, making short, shallow submersions after each blow. The fin-whale is a comparatively slim creature as whales go, but one of these exposed a bulk of back that suggested to the whaleman's mind a vision of at least sixty barrels (ten tons) of oil.

" Take *him*! " shouted Svendsen from the wheel, and steered accordingly.

For a stern chase it was a short one. At half speed the *Thorgrim* overhauled its quarry, steaming parallel with the latter's course. Now the whales rose barely fifty fathoms ahead; now they could be perceived under water, off the starboard bow. Gradually the shadowy giant shapes became distinct as they lifted obliquely to the surface. The *Thorgrim's* propeller stopped; she slid forward silently, describing a curve so that when the whales reached the surface they should cross her bows. Unsuspicious of danger, they came lazily into the position desired.

Sigurd saw only the nearer whale, the great sixty-barrel *finhval*. His nerves were strung to a high pitch. To fire too soon was even worse than to fire too late; for while the harpoon would hold in a non-vital part of the body, and the chance of ultimate capture remain, it would almost certainly rebound from the head, with fragments of the bomb scattering in all directions.

Gradually the crown of the head broke water with a drowsy-sounding blast, and as calmly sank in front of the bulging shoulders, which appeared to roll forward followed by the swelling back and blue-grey flanks, whence the brine ran greasily. Sigurd, wound up like a steel spring, waited—waited until he was offered his target in an imaginary point six or seven feet abaft the pectoral fin. Then he let fly. And in the same instant he seemed to go blind.

" Did I strike him? " he cried, wheeling about and appealing to no one in particular, oblivious of the gust of spray that drenched him, the rushing cable, the yell

64

of congratulation from his skipper, who had seen the harpoon flash to the butt in the whale's side. " Did I strike him? " Abruptly he stepped from the platform and sat down on its edge, laughing foolishly.

" Sigurd! " Svendsen bawled, " look out! "

That brought him to himself, and the clank of the winch acted like a spur. At once he was up and on duty, watching the cable, giving orders to winchman and steersman, helping to reload the gun.

The cable halted in its rapid running, and went out in spasmodic and rather feeble jerks. The winch was braked, and the hemp became taut, yet not severely strained. The *Thorgrim* began to back gently, coaxingly.

At the end of five minutes the whale came up and blew violently. Remaining at the surface, half a cable's length from the steamer, with scarce a motion, he continued to blow almost without pause. Suddenly it was seen that his exhaust breath was pinkish. A minute later it was a crimson rain.

Hansen, the cook, clapped Sigurd on the back. " I could not have done better myself," said he. " I think Johan has lost his three *kroner*."

" Bah! giddy old gunner of rabbits! " said Johan, " I do not grudge Sigurd the three *kroner*. It was a great shot, and to show you that I have a generous mind, Hansen, I will tell you for nothing how you may kill your rabbits quicker than with a gun."

" How shall I do that, Johan? "

" Cook for them! "

" Look out! " cried Sigurd sharply. " Let go! "

The whale had made a wild rush away from the

Thorgrim, and the winchman unbraked just in time.

" It is the finish," he remarked. " I will give you the three *kroner,* Sigurd, when——" He stopped short, his mouth open.

The whale had turned about, buried his head, flung out his tail and a third of his body, and executed a complete somersault.

" *Gud!* " whispered the cook, " I never saw a *finhval* do that before." Nor, probably, had anyone on board the *Thorgrim.*

" Sigurd! Give him plenty of line," shouted Svendsen, as the whale stood upright in the sea, his gaping jaws, toothless, but bristling with short baleen, clear of the water.

The *Thorgrim* backed at increased speed, and the cable was allowed to run forth until its length was nearly exhausted. Whereupon the engines were stopped and the winch was braked again. The whale bobbed awhile in painfully grotesque fashion, then all at once began literally to waltz towards the steamer, winding the cable about his body.

Once more the *Thorgrim* was sent astern. Sigurd glanced at his skipper's face, and saw anxiety there. Why did not the creature die? The shot had undoubtedly reached the lungs. It was unusual behaviour for a rorqual, whether wounded slightly or vitally. The pull of the cable, however, had the desired effect; the waltzing came to an end, and the whale, returning to the horizontal, rolled heavily over and over until the coils were unwound from his body. For a long minute's space he lay perfectly still.

Sigurd drew a breath of relief, and almost immediately the whale blew an appalling gust of crimson, and sounded. The cable ripped the water towards the *Thorgrim,* which was lying-to, and before she could be got under way the whale was up again—within fifty fathoms of her—lashing the sea to froth, and blowing with a horrible sound.

" *Now* he is finished," Johan muttered, reeling in the slack at top speed.

As he spoke the whale made a forward dash and drove at the enemy like a torpedo.

" More speed! " Svendsen snapped down the tube, and the steamer throbbed hard astern. " My God! " he muttered, " he has got us! "

A queer ghastliness came into the brown faces of all on deck. Possessed by some premonition, the cook grabbed Sigurd's arm and hauled him, staggering, abaft the mast.

Even as he did so the whale, rushing on the port bow, flung head and shoulders out of the sea. There was a flash of the dazzlingly white grooved under-body, and then, amidst a shower of blood, the lower jaw crashed across the bows, crumpling rails, bursting stays, flattening the fo'c'sle chimney.

The *Thorgrim* heeled over until men sprawled and made sure that she was turning turtle—until the whale slid backwards and dropped with an awful plunge—dead!

J. J. BELL—*The Whale Hunters.*

A VERY DESPERATE VENTURE

The Doones lived in a lonely valley in North Devon. Their chief, Sir Ensor Doone, had been outlawed and their valley was always carefully guarded. John Ridd, a young farmer, had no reason to love these Doones for they had murdered his father. When he was about fourteen years old he had climbed Bagworthy Water into the territory of the Doones and seen Lorna, granddaughter of Sir Ensor. In years to come Lorna and John met frequently in secret and they had a series of signals by which John might know that all was well with Lorna. When these signals suddenly ceased John resolved on the very desperate venture described in the following extract.

John tells the story.

A VERY DESPERATE VENTURE

That the enterprise now resolved upon was far more
dangerous than any hitherto attempted by me, needs no
further proof than this:—I went and made my will at
Porlock, with a middling honest lawyer there; not that
I had much to leave, but that none could say how far
the farm, and all the farming stock, might depend on
my disposition. It makes me smile when I remember
how particular I was, and how for the life of me I was
puzzled to bequeath most part of my clothes and hats,
and things altogether my own, to Lorna, without the
shrewd old lawyer knowing who she was, and where she
lived. At last, indeed, I flattered myself that I had
baffled old Tape's curiosity; but his wrinkled smile,
and his speech at parting, made me again uneasy.

"A very excellent will, young sir. An admirably
just and virtuous will; all your effects to your nearest

of kin; filial and fraternal duty thoroughly exemplified; nothing diverted to alien channels, except a small token of esteem and reverence to an elderly lady, I presume: and which may or may not be valid, or invalid, on the ground of uncertainty, or the absence of any legal status on the part of the legatee. Ha, ha! Yes, yes! Few young men are so free from undesirable entanglements. Two guineas is my charge, sir: and a rare good will for the money. Very prudent of you, sir. Does you credit in every way. Well, well: we all must die; and often the young before the old."

Not only did I think two guineas a great deal too much money for a quarter of an hour's employment, but also I disliked particularly the words with which he concluded: they sounded, from his grating voice, like the evil omen of a croaking raven. Nevertheless I still abode in my fixed resolve to go, and find out, if I died for it, what was become of Lorna. And herein I lay no claim to courage; the matter being simply a choice between two evils, of which by far the greater one was, of course, to lose my darling.

The journey was a great deal longer to fetch around the Southern hills, and enter by the Doone-gate, than to cross the lower land, and steal in by the water-slide. However, I durst not take a horse (for fear of the Doones, who might be abroad upon their usual business) but started betimes in the evening, so as not to hurry, or waste any strength upon the way. And thus I came to the robbers' highway, walking circumspectly, scanning the sky-line of every hill, and searching the folds of every valley, for any moving figure.

Although it was now well on towards dark, and the

sun was down an hour or so, I could see the robbers'
road before me, in a trough of the winding hills, where
the brook ploughed down from the higher barrows,
and the coving banks were roofed with furze. At
present, there was no one passing, neither post nor
sentinel, so far as I could descry; but I thought it safer
to wait a little, as twilight melted into night; and then
I crept down a seam of the highland, and stood upon
the Doone-track.

As the road approached the entrance, it became more
straight and strong, like a channel cut from rock, with
the water brawling darkly along the naked side of it.
Not a tree or bush was left, to shelter a man from
bullets: all was stern, and stiff, and rugged, as I could
not help perceiving, even through the darkness; and a
smell as of churchyard mould, a sense of being boxed
in and cooped, made me long to be out again.

And here I was, or seemed to be, particularly unlucky;
for as I drew near the very entrance, lightly of foot, and
warily, the moon (which had often been my friend)
like an enemy broke upon me, topping the eastward
ridge of rock, and filling all the open spaces with the
play of wavering light. I shrank back into the shadowy
quarter, on the right side of the road; and gloomily
employed myself to watch the triple entrance, on which
the moonlight fell askew.

All across and before the three rude and beetling
archways, hung a felled oak overhead, black, and thick,
and threatening. This, as I heard before, could be let
fall in a moment, so as to crush a score of men, and
bar the approach of horses. Behind this tree, the rocky
mouth was spanned, as by a gallery, with brushwood

and piled timber, all upon a ledge of stone, where thirty men might lurk unseen, and fire at any invader. From that rampart it would be impossible to dislodge them, because the rock fell sheer below them twenty feet, or it may be more; while overhead it towered three hundred, and so jutted over that nothing could be cast upon them; even if a man could climb the height. And the access to this portcullis place—if I may so call it, being no portcullis there—was through certain rocky chambers known to the tenants only.

But the cleverest of their devices, and the most puzzling to an enemy, was that, instead of one mouth only, there were three to choose from, with nothing to betoken which was the proper access; all being pretty much alike, and all unfenced and yawning. And the common rumour was that in times of any danger, when any force was known to be on muster in their neighbourhood, they changed their entrance every day, and diverted the other two, by means of sliding doors, to the chasms and dark abysses.

Now I could see those three rough arches, jagged, black, and terrible; and I knew that only one of them could lead me to the valley; neither gave the river now any further guidance, but dived underground with a sullen roar, where it met the cross-bar of the mountain. Having no means at all of judging which was the right way of the three, and knowing that the other two would lead to almost certain death, in the ruggedness and darkness—for how could a man, among precipices and bottomless depths of water, without a ray of light, have any chance to save his life?—I do declare that I was half inclined to go away, and have done with it.

However, I knew one thing for certain, to wit, that the longer I stayed debating, the more would the enterprise pall upon me, and the less my relish be. And it struck me that, in times of peace, the middle way was the likeliest; and the others diverging right and left in their further parts might be made to slide into it (not far from the entrance), at the pleasure of the warders. Also I took it for good omen that I remembered (as rarely happened) a very fine line in the Latin grammar, whose emphasis and meaning is "middle road is safest."

Therefore, without more hesitation, I plunged into the middle way, holding a long ash staff before me, shodden at the end with iron. Presently I was in black darkness, groping along the wall, and feeling a deal more fear than I wished to feel; especially when upon looking back I could no longer see the light, which I had forsaken. Then I stumbled over something hard, and sharp, and very cold, moreover so grievous to my legs, that it needed my very best doctrine and humour to forbear from swearing in the manner they use in London. But when I arose, and felt it, and knew it to be a culverin, I was somewhat reassured thereby, inasmuch as it was not likely that they would plant this engine, except in the real and true entrance.

Therefore I went on again, more painfully and wearily, and presently found it to be good that I had received this knock, and borne it with such patience; for otherwise I might have blundered full upon the sentries, and been shot without more ado. As it was, I had barely time to draw back, as I turned a corner upon them; and if their lanthorn had been in its place, they could scarce have failed to descry me, unless indeed I had seen the gleam before I turned the corner.

There seemed to be only two of them, of size indeed and stature as all the Doones must be, but I need not have feared to encounter them both, had they been unarmed, as I was. It was plain, however, that each had a long and heavy carbine, not in his hands (as it should have been), but standing close beside him. Therefore it behoved me now to be exceedingly careful; and even that might scarce avail, without luck in proportion. So I kept well back at the corner, and laid one cheek to the rock face, and kept my outer eye round the jut, in the wariest mode I could compass, watching my opportunity: and this is what I saw.

The two villains looked very happy—which villains have no right to be, but often are, meseemeth—they were sitting in a niche of rock, with a lanthorn in the corner, quaffing something from glass measures, and playing at push-pin, or shepherd's chess, or basset; or some trivial game of that sort. Each was smoking a long clay pipe, quite of new London shape I could see, for the shadow was thrown out clearly; and each would laugh from time to time, as he fancied he got the better of it. One was sitting with his knees up, and left hand on his thigh, and this one had his back to me, and seemed to be the stouter. The other leaned more against the rock, half sitting and half astraddle, and wearing leathern overalls, as if newly come from riding. I could see his face quite clearly by the light of the open lanthorn, and a handsomer or a bolder face I had seldom, if ever, set eyes upon; insomuch that it made me very unhappy to think of his being so near my Lorna.

"How long am I to stay crouching here?" I asked of myself at last, being tired of hearing them cry, "score one," "score two," "No, by——, Charlie," "By——I say it is, Phelps." And yet my only chance of slipping by them unperceived was to wait till they quarrelled more, and came to blows about it. Presently, as I made up my mind to steal along towards them (for the cavern was pretty wide, just there), Charlie, or Charleworth Doone, the younger and taller man, reached forth his hand to seize the money, which he swore he had won that time. Upon this, the other jerked his arm, vowing that he had no right to it; whereupon Charlie flung at his face the contents of the glass he was sipping, but missed him and hit the candle, which spluttered with a flare of blue flame (from the strength, perhaps, of the spirit) and then went out completely. At this, one swore, and the other laughed; and before they had settled what to do, I was past them and round the corner.

And then, like a giddy fool as I was, I needs must give them a startler—the whoop of an owl, done so exactly, as John Fry had taught me, and echoed by the roof, so fearfully, that one of them dropped the tinder box, and the other caught up his gun and cocked it, at least as I judged by the sounds they made. And then, too late, I knew by my madness, for if either of them had fired, no doubt but what all the village would have risen, and rushed upon me. However, as the luck of the matter went, it proved for my advantage; for I heard one say to the other,—

"Curse it, Charlie, what was that? It scared me so, I have dropped my box; my flint is gone, and everything. Will the brimstone catch from your pipe, my lad?"

"My pipe is out, Phelps, ever so long. Damn it, I am not afraid of an owl, man. Give me the lanthorn, and stay here. I'm not half-done with you yet, my friend."

"Well said, my boy, well said! Go straight to Carver's, mind you. The other sleepy-heads be snoring, as there is nothing up to-night. No dallying now under Captain's window. Queen will have nought to say to you; and Carver will punch your head into a new wick for your lanthorn."

"Will he though? Two can play at that." And so after some rude jests, and laughter, and a few more oaths, I heard Charlie (or at any rate somebody) coming toward me, with a loose and not too sober footfall. As he reeled a little in his gait, and I would not move from his way one inch, after his talk of Lorna, but only longed to grasp him (if common sense permitted it), his braided coat came against my thumb, and his leathern gaiters brushed my knee. If he had turned or noticed it, he would have been a dead man in a moment; but his drunkenness saved him.

So I let him reel on unharmed; and thereupon it occurred to me that I could have no better guide, passing as he would exactly where I wished to be; that is to say under Lorna's window. Therefore I followed him, without any especial caution; and soon I had the pleasure of seeing his form against the moonlit sky. Down a steep and winding path, with a handrail at the corners (such as they have at Ilfracombe), Master

Charlie tripped along—and indeed there was much tripping, and he must have been an active fellow to recover as he did—and after him walked I, much hoping (for his own poor sake) that he might not turn, and espy me.

But Bacchus (of whom I read at school, with great wonder about his meaning—and the same I may say of Venus) that great deity preserved Charlie, his pious worshipper, from regarding consequences. So he led me very kindly to the top of the meadow land, where the stream from underground broke forth, seething quietly with a little hiss of bubbles. Hence I had fair view and outline of the robbers' township, spread with bushes here and there, but not heavily overshadowed. The moon, approaching now the full, brought the forms in manner forth, clothing each with character, as the moon (more than the sun) does, to an eye accustomed.

I knew that the Captain's house was first, both from what Lorna had said of it, and from my mother's description, and now again from seeing Charlie halt there for a certain time, and whistle on his fingers, and and hurry on, fearing consequences. The tune that he whistled was strange to me, and lingered in my ears, as having something very new and striking, and fantastic in it. And I repeated it softly to myself, while I marked the position of the houses and the beauty of the village. For the stream, in lieu of any street, passing between the houses, and affording perpetual change, and twinkling, and reflections, moreover by its sleepy murmur soothing all the dwellers there, this and the snugness of the position, walled with rock and spread like herbage, made it look, in the quiet moonlight, like a little paradise. And to think of all the inmates there, sleeping with good consciences, having plied their useful trade of making others work for them, enjoying life without much labour, yet with great renown!

Master Charlie went down the village, and I followed him carefully, keeping as much as possible in the shadowy places, and watching the windows of every house, lest any light should be burning. As I passed Sir Ensor's house, my heart leaped up, for I spied a window, higher than the rest above the ground, and with a faint light moving. This could hardly fail to be the room wherein my darling lay; for here that impudent young fellow had gazed while he was whistling. And here my courage grew tenfold, and my spirit feared no evil—for lo, if Lorna had been surrendered to that scoundrel, Carver, she would not have been at her grandfather's house, but in Carver's accursed dwelling.

Warm with this idea, I hurried after Charleworth Doone, being resolved not to harm him now, unless my own life required it. And while I watched from behind a tree, the door of the furthest house was opened; and sure enough it was Carver's self, who stood bare-headed, and half-undressed, in the doorway. I could see his great black chest, and arms, by the light of the lamp he bore.

"Who wants me, this time of night?" he grumbled in a deep gruff voice; "any young scamp prowling after the maids shall have sore bones for his trouble."

"All the fair maids are for thee, are they, Master Carver?" Charlie answered, laughing: "we young

78

scamps must be well-content with coarser stuff than thou wouldst have."

"Would have? Ay, and will have," the great beast muttered angrily. "I bide my time; but not very long. Only one word for thy good, Charlie. I will fling thee senseless into the river, if ever I catch thy girl-face there again."

"Mayhap, Master Carver, it is more than thou couldst do. But I will not keep thee; thou art not pleasant company to-night. All I want is a light for my lanthorn, and a glass of schnapps, if thou hast it."

"What is become of thy light, then? Good for thee I am not on duty."

"A great owl flew between me and Phelps, as we watched beside the culverin, and so scared was he at our fierce bright eyes, that he fell, and knocked the light out."

"Likely tale, or likely lie, Charles! We will have the truth to-morrow. Here, take thy light, and be gone with thee. All virtuous men are in bed now."

"Then so will I be, and why art thou not? Ha, have I not earned my schnapps now?"

"If thou hast, thou hast paid a bad debt: there is too much in thee already. Be off! my patience is done with."

Then he slammed the door in the young man's face, having kindled his lanthorn by this time: and Charlie went up to the watch-place again, muttering as he passed me, "Bad look-out for all of us, when that surly old beast is Captain. No gentle blood in him, no hospitality, not even pleasant language, nor a good new oath in his frowsy pate! I've a mind to cut the whole of it; and but for the girls I would do so."

My heart was in my mouth, as they say, when I stood in the shade by Lorna's window, and whispered her name gently. The house was of one storey only, as the others were, with pine-ends standing forth the stone, and only two rough windows upon that western side of it, and perhaps both of them were Lorna's. The Doones had been their own builders, for no one should know their ins and outs; and of course their work was clumsy. As for their windows, they stole them mostly from the houses round about. But though the window was not very close, I might have whispered long enough, before she would have answered me; frightened as she was, no doubt, by many a rude overture. And I durst not speak aloud, because I saw another watchman posted on the western cliff, and commanding all the valley. And now this man (having no companion for drinking or for gambling) espied me against the wall of the house, and advanced to the brink, and challenged me.

"Who are you there? Answer! One, two, three; and I fire at thee."

The nozzle of his gun was pointed full upon me, as I could see, with the moonlight striking on the barrel; he was not more than fifty yards off, and now he began to reckon. Being almost desperate about it, I began to whistle, wondering how far I should get before I lost my windpipe: and as luck would have it, my lips fell into that strange tune I had practised last; the one I had heard from Charlie. My mouth would scarcely frame the notes, being parched with terror; but to my surprise, the man fell back, dropped his gun, and saluted. Oh, sweetest of all sweet melodies!

That tune was Carver Doone's passport (as I heard long afterwards), which Charleworth Doone had imitated, for decoy of Lorna. The sentinel took me for that vile Carver; who was like enough to be prowling there, for private talk with Lorna; but not very likely to shout forth his name, if it might be avoided. The watchman, perceiving the danger perhaps of intruding on Carver's privacy, not only retired along the cliffs, but withdrew himself to good distance.

Meanwhile he had done me the kindest service; for Lorna came to the window at once, to see what the cause of the shout was, and drew back the curtain timidly. Then she opened the rough lattice; and then she watched the cliff and trees; and then she sighed very sadly.

"Oh, Lorna, don't you know me? " I whispered from the side, being afraid of startling her by appearing over suddenly.

Quick though she always was of thought, she knew me not from my whisper, and was shutting the window hastily, when I caught it back, and showed myself.

"John! " she cried, yet with sense enough not to speak aloud: "Oh, you must be mad, John."

"As mad as a March hare," said I, "without any news of my darling. You knew I would come; of course you did."

"Well, I thought, perhaps——you know: now, John, you need not eat my hand. Do you see they have put iron bars across? "

"To be sure. Do you think I should be contented,

even with this lovely hand, but for these vile iron bars?
I will have them out before I go. Now, darling, for
one moment—just the other hand, for a change, you
know."

So I got the other, but was not honest; for I kept
them both, and felt their delicate beauty trembling, as
I laid them to my heart.

"Oh, John, you will make me cry directly"—she
had been crying long ago—"if you go on in that way.
You know we can never have one another; everyone
is against it. Why should I make you miserable? Try
not to think of me any more."

"And will you try the same of me, Lorna?"

"Oh, yes, John; if you agree to it. At least I will
try to try it."

"Then you won't try anything of the sort," I cried
with great enthusiasm, for her tone was so nice and
melancholy: "the only thing we will try to try, is to
belong to one another. And if we do our best, Lorna,
God alone can prevent us."

She crossed herself, with one hand drawn free, as I
spoke so boldly: and something swelled in her little
throat, and prevented her from answering.

"Now tell me," I said; "what means all this? Why
are you so pent up here? Why have you given me no
token? Has your grandfather turned against you? Are
you in any danger?"

"My poor grandfather is very ill: I fear that he will
not live long. The Counsellor and his son are now the
masters of the valley; and I dare not venture forth, for
fear of anything they might do to me. When I went
forth, to signal for you, Carver tried to seize me; but I

was too quick for him. Little Gwenny is not allowed to leave the valley now; so that I could send no message. I have been so wretched, dear, lest you should think me false to you. The tyrants now make sure of me. You must watch this house, both night and day, if you wish to save me. There is nothing they would shrink from, if my poor grandfather—oh, I cannot bear to think of myself, when I ought to think of him only; dying without a son to tend him, or a daughter to shed a tear."

"But surely he has sons enough; and a deal too many," I was going to say, but stopped myself in time: "why do none of them come to him?"

"I know not. I cannot tell. He is a very strange old man; and few have ever loved him. He was black with wrath at the Counsellor, this very afternoon—but I must not keep you here—you are much too brave, John; and I am much too selfish: there, what was that shadow?"

"Nothing more than a bat, darling, come to look for his sweetheart. I will not stay long; you tremble so: and yet for that very same reason, how can I leave you, Lorna?"

"You must—you must," she answered; "I shall die if they hurt you. I hear the old nurse moving. Grandfather is sure to send for me. Keep back from the window."

However, it was only Gwenny Carfax, Lorna's little handmaid: my darling brought her to the window, and presented her to me, almost laughing through her grief.

"Oh, I am so glad, John; Gwenny, I am so glad you

came. I have wanted long to introduce you to my
' young man,' as you call him. It is rather dark, but
you can see him. I wish you to know him again,
Gwenny."

" Whoy! " cried Gwenny, with great amazement,
standing on tiptoe to look out, and staring as if she
were weighing me: " her be bigger nor any Doone!
Heared as her have bate our Carnish champion awrast-
ling. 'Twadn't fair play nohow: no, no; don't tell me,
'twadn't fair play nohow."

" True enough, Gwenny," I answered her; for the
play had been very unfair indeed on the side of the
Bodmin champion: " it was not a fair bout, little maid;
I am free to acknowledge that." By that answer, or
rather by the construction she put upon it, the heart
of the Cornish girl was won, more than by gold and
silver.

" I shall knoo thee again, young man; no fear of
that," she answered, nodding with an air of patronage.
" Now, missis, gae on coortin', and I wall gae outside
and watch for 'ee." Though expressed not over
delicately, this proposal arose, no doubt, from Gwenny's
sense of delicacy; and I was very thankful to her for
taking her departure.

" She is the best little thing in the world," said Lorna,
softly laughing; " and the queerest, and the truest.
Nothing will bribe her against me. If she seems to be
on the other side, never, never doubt her. Now no
more of your ' coortin',' John! I love you far too well
for that. Yes, yes, ever so much! If you will take a
mean advantage of me. As much as ever you like to
imagine; and then you may double it, after that. Only

go, do go, good John; kind, dear, darling John; if you love me, go."

" How can I go, without settling anything? " I asked, very sensibly. "How shall I know of your danger now? Hit upon something; you are so quick. Anything you can think of; and then I will go, and not frighten you."

" I have been thinking long of something," Lorna answered rapidly, with that peculiar clearness of voice, which made every syllable ring like music of a several note; "you see that tree with the seven rooks' nests, bright against the cliffs there? Can you count them, from above, do you think? From a place where you will be safe, dear "——

" No doubt, I can; or if I cannot, it will not take me long to find a spot whence I can do it."

"Gwenny can climb like any cat. She has been up there in the summer, watching the young birds, day by day, and daring the boys to touch them. There are neither birds nor eggs there now, of course, and nothing doing. If you see but six rooks' nests, I am in peril, and want you. If you see but five, I am carried off by Carver."

" Good God! " said I, at the mere idea, in a tone which frightened Lorna.

" Fear not, John," she whispered sadly, and my blood grew cold at it: "I have means to stop him; or at least to save myself. If you can come within one day of that man's getting hold of me, you will find me quite unharmed. After that you will find me dead, or alive, according to circumstances, but in no case such that you need blush to look at me."

85

Her dear sweet face was full of pride, as even in the gloom I saw: and I would not trespass on her feelings, by such a thing, at such a moment, as an attempt at any caress. I only said, "God bless you, darling!" and she said the same to me, in a very low sad voice. And then I stole below Carver's house, in the shadow from the eastern cliff; and knowing enough of the village now to satisfy all necessity, betook myself to my well-known track in returning from the valley; which was neither down the water-slide (a course I feared in the darkness) nor up the cliffs at Lorna's bower; but a way of my own inventing, which there is no need to dwell upon.

A weight of care was off my mind; though much of trouble hung there still. One thing was quite certain— if Lorna could not have John Ridd, no one else should have her. And my mother, who sat up for me, and with me long time afterwards, agreed that this was comfort.

R. D. BLACKMORE.—*Lorna Doone.*

CARTON'S SACRIFICE

THE main incidents in this story take place in Paris in the days of the Revolution. The Marquis St. Evrémonde has been living in England under the name of Charles Darnay, in which name he had married Lucie Manette, daughter of Dr. Manette, who had been a prisoner in the Bastille for eighteen years. When the steward of the Evrémonde estates appeals by letter to the Marquis to secure his release from prison, Darnay journeys to Paris. He is, however, recognized as an aristocrat, tried and condemned to the guillotine. His wife and Dr. Manette hasten to Paris, but it is an Englishman, Sydney Carton, who has long loved Lucie, who, as the extract describes, finally effects a rescue.

CARTON'S SACRIFICE

THE hours went on as he walked to and fro, and the clocks struck the numbers he would never hear again. Nine gone for ever, ten gone for ever, eleven gone for ever, twelve coming on to pass away. After a hard contest with that eccentric action of thought which had last perplexed him, he had got the better of it. He walked up and down, softly repeating their names to himself. The worst of the strife was over. He could walk up and down, free from distracting fancies, praying for himself and for them.

Twelve gone for ever.

He had been apprised that the final hour was three, and he knew he would be summoned some time earlier, inasmuch as the tumbrils jolted heavily and slowly through the streets. Therefore, he resolved to keep two before his mind, as the hour, and so to strengthen himself in the interval that he might be able, after that time, to strengthen others.

Walking regularly to and fro with his arms folded on his breast, a very different man from the prisoner who had walked to and fro at La Force, he heard one struck away from him, without surprise. The hour had measured like most other hours. Devoutly thankful to Heaven for his recovered self-possession, he thought, "There is but another now," and turned to walk again.

Footsteps in the stone passage, outside the door. He stopped.

The key was put in the lock, and turned. Before the door was opened, or as it opened, a man said in a low voice, in English, "He has never seen me here; I have kept out of his way. Go you in alone; I wait near. Lose no time!"

The door was quickly opened and closed, and there stood before him, face to face, quiet, intent upon him, with the light of a smile on his features and a cautionary finger on his lip, Sydney Carton.

There was something so bright and remarkable in his look, that, for the first moment, the prisoner misdoubted him to be an apparition of his own imagining. But he spoke, and it was his voice; he took the prisoner's hand, and it was his real grasp.

"Of all the people upon earth, you least expected to see me?" he said.

"I could not believe it to be you. I can scarcely believe it now. You are not"—the apprehension came suddenly into his mind—"a prisoner?"

"No. I am accidentally possessed of a power over

one of the keepers here, and in virtue of it I stand before you. I come from her—your wife, dear Darnay."

The prisoner wrung his hand.

"I bring you a request from her."

"What is it?"

"A most earnest, pressing, and emphatic entreaty, addressed to you in the most pathetic tones of the voice so dear to you, that you well remember."

The prisoner turned his face partly aside.

"You have no time to ask me why I bring it, or what it means; I have no time to tell you. You must comply with it—take off those boots you wear, and draw on these of mine."

There was a chair against the wall of the cell, behind the prisoner. Carton, pressing forward, had already, with the speed of lightning, got him down into it, and stood over him barefoot.

"Draw on these boots of mine. Put your hands to them; put your will to them. Quick!"

"Carton, there is no escaping from this place; it never can be done. You will only die with me. It is madness."

"It would be madness if I asked you to escape; but do I? When I ask you to pass out at that door, tell me it is madness and remain here. Change that cravat for this of mine, that coat for this of mine. While you do it, let me take this ribbon from your hair, and shake out your hair like this of mine!"

With wonderful quickness, and with a strength, both of will and action, that appeared quite supernatural, he forced all these changes upon him. The prisoner was like a young child in his hands.

" Carton! Dear Carton! It is madness. It cannot be accomplished, it never can be done, it has been attempted, and has always failed. I implore you not to add your death to the bitterness of mine."

" Do I ask you, my dear Darnay, to pass the door? When I ask you that, refuse. There are pen and ink and paper on this table. Is your hand steady enough to write? "

" It was, when you came in."

" Steady it again, and write what I shall dictate. Quick, friend, quick! "

Pressing his hand to his bewildered head, Darnay sat down at the table. Carton, with his right hand in his breast, stood close beside him.

" Write exactly as I speak."

" To whom do I address it? "

" To no one." Carton still had his hand in his breast.

" Do I date it? "

" No."

The prisoner looked up, at each question. Carton, standing over him with his hand in his breast, looked down.

" 'If you remember,' " said Carton, dictating, " ' the words that passed between us, long ago, you will readily comprehend this when you see it. You do remember them, I know. It is not in your nature to forget them.' "

He was drawing his hand from his breast; the prisoner chancing to look up in his hurried wonder as he wrote, the hand stopped, closing upon something.

" Have you written ' forget them '? " Carton asked.

"I have. Is that a weapon in your hand?"

"No; I am not armed."

"What is it in your hand?"

"You shall know directly. Write on; there are but a few words more." He dictated again. "'I am thankful that the time has come when I can prove them. That I do so is no subject for regret or grief.'" As he said these words, with his eyes fixed on the writer, his hand slowly and softly moved down close to the writer's face.

The pen dropped from Darnay's fingers on the table and he looked about him vacantly.

"What vapour is that?" he asked.

"Vapour?"

"Something that crossed me?"

"I am conscious of nothing; there can be nothing here. Take up the pen and finish. Hurry, hurry!"

As if his memory were impaired, or his faculties disordered, the prisoner made an effort to rally his attention. As he looked at Carton with clouded eyes and with an altered manner of breathing, Carton—his hand again in his breast—looked steadily at him.

"Hurry, hurry!"

The prisoner bent over the paper once more.

"'If it had been otherwise'"—Carton's hand was again watchfully and softly stealing down—"'I never should have used the longer opportunity. If it had been otherwise"'—the hand was at the prisoner's face—"'I should but have had so much the more to answer for. If it had been otherwise——'" Carton looked at the pen, and saw that it was trailing off into unintelligible signs.

Carton's hand moved back to his breast no more. The prisoner sprang up, with a reproachful look, but Carton's hand was close and firm at his nostrils, and Carton's left arm caught him round the waist. For a few seconds he faintly struggled with the man who had come to lay down his life for him; but within a minute or so, he was stretched insensible on the ground.

Quickly, but with hands as true to the purpose as his heart was, Carton dressed himself in the clothes the prisoner had laid aside, combed back his hair, and tied it with ribbon the prisoner had worn. Then he softly called, " Enter there! Come in! " and the spy presented himself.

" You see? " said Carton, looking up, as he kneeled on one knee beside the insensible figure, putting the paper in the breast; " is your hazard very great? "

" Mr. Carton," the spy answered, with a timid snap of his fingers, " my hazard is not *that*, in the thick of business here, if you are true to the whole of your bargain."

" Don't fear me. I will be true to the death."

" You must be, Mr. Carton, if the tale of fifty-two is to be right. Being made right by you in that dress, I shall have no fear."

" Have no fear! I shall soon be out of the way of harming you, and the rest will soon be far from here, please God! Now, get assistance and take me to the coach."

" You? " said the spy nervously.

" Him, man, with whom I have exchanged. You go out at the gate by which you brought me in? "

" Of course."

" I was weak and faint when you brought me in, and I am fainter now you take me out. The parting interview has overpowered me. Such a thing has happened here often, and too often. Your life is in your own hands. Quick! Call assistance! "

" You swear not to betray me? " said the trembling spy, as he paused for a last moment.

" Man, man! " returned Carton, stamping his foot; " have I sworn by no solemn vow already, to go through with this, that you waste the precious moments now? Take him yourself to the courtyard you know of, place him yourself in the carriage, show him yourself to Mr. Lorry, tell him yourself to give him no restorative but air, and to remember my words of last night and his promise of last night, and drive away! "

The spy withdrew, and Carton seated himself at the table, resting his forehead on his hands. The spy returned immediately, with two men.

" How, then? " said one of them, contemplating the fallen figure. " So afflicted to find that his friend has drawn a prize in the lottery of Saint Guillotine? "

" A good patriot," said the other, " could hardly have been more afflicted if the aristocrat had drawn a blank."

They raised the unconscious figure, placed it on a litter they had brought to the door, and bent to carry it away.

" The time is short, Evrémonde," said the spy, in a warning voice.

" I know it well," answered Carton. " Be careful of my friend, I entreat you, and leave me."

" Come, then, my children," said Barsad. " Lift him, and come away! "

The door closed, and Carton was left alone. Straining his powers of listening to the utmost, he listened for any sound that might denote suspicion or alarm. There was none. Keys turned, doors clashed, footsteps passed along distant passages: no cry was raised, or hurry made, that seemed unusual. Breathing more freely in a little while, he sat down at the table, and listened again until the clocks struck two.

Sounds that he was not afraid of, for he divined their meaning, then began to be audible. Several doors were opened in quick succession, and finally his own. A jailer, with a list in his hand, looked in, merely saying, " Follow me, Evrémonde! " and he followed into a large dark room, at a distance. It was a dark winter day, and what with the shadows within, and what with the shadows without, he could but dimly discern the others who were brought there to have their arms bound. Some were standing; some seated. Some were lamenting, and in restless motion; but these were few. The great majority were silent and still, looking fixedly at the ground.

As he stood by the wall in a dim corner, while some of the fifty-two were brought in after him, one man stopped in passing, to embrace him, as having a knowledge of him. It thrilled him with a great dread of discovery; but the man went on. A very few moments after that, a young woman, with a slight girlish form, a sweet spare face in which there was no vestige of colour, and large, widely-opened, patient eyes, rose from the seat where he had observed her sitting, and came to speak to him.

"Citizen Evrémonde," she said, touching him with her cold hand. "I am a poor little seamstress, who was with you in La Force."

He murmured for answer: "True. I forget what you were accused of?"

"Plots. Though the just Heaven knows I am innocent of any. Is it likely? Who would think of plotting with a poor little weak creature like me?"

The forlorn smile with which she said it, so touched him, that tears started from his eyes.

"I am not afraid to die, Citizen Evrémonde, but I have done nothing. I am not unwilling to die, if the Republic which is to do so much good to us poor, will profit by my death; but I do not know how that can be, Citizen Evrémonde. Such a poor weak little creature!"

As the last thing on earth that his heart was to warm and soften to, it warmed and softened to this pitiable girl.

"I heard you were released, Citizen Evrémonde. I hoped it was true?"

"It was. But I was again taken and condemned."

"If I may ride with you, Citizen Evrémonde, will you let me hold your hand? I am not afraid, but I am little and weak, and it will give me more courage."

As the patient eyes were lifted to his face, he saw a sudden doubt in them, and then astonishment. He pressed the work-worn, hunger-worn young fingers, and touched his lips.

"Are you dying for him?" she whispered.

" And his wife and child. Hush! Yes."

" Oh, you will let me hold your brave hand, stranger? "

" Hush! Yes, my poor sister; to the last."

The same shadows that are falling on the prison, are falling, in that same hour of the early afternoon, on the barrier with the crowd about it, when a coach going out of Paris drives up to be examined.

" Who goes here? Whom have we within? Papers! " The papers are handed out, and read.

" Alexandre Manette. Physician. French. Which is he? "

This is he; this helpless, inarticulately murmuring, wandering old man pointed out.

" Apparently the citizen-doctor is not in his right mind? The revolution-fever will have been too much for him? "

Greatly too much for him.

" Hah! Many suffer with it. Lucie. His daughter. French. Which is she? "

This is she.

" Apparently it must be. Lucie, the wife of Evrémonde; is it not? "

It is.

" Hah! Evrémonde has an assignation elsewhere. Lucie, her child. English. This is she? "

She and no other.

" Kiss me, child of Evrémonde. Now, thou hast kissed a good Republican; something new in thy family; remember it! Sydney Carton. Advocate. English. Which is he? "

He lies here, in this corner of the carriage. He, too, is pointed out.

"Apparently the English advocate is in a swoon?"

It is hoped he will recover in the fresher air. It is represented that he is not in strong health, and has separated sadly from a friend who is under the displeasure of the Republic.

"Is that all? It is not a great deal, that! Many are under the displeasure of the Republic, and must look out at the little window. Jarvis Lorry. Banker. English. Which is he?"

"I am he. Necessarily, being the last."

It is Jarvis Lorry who has replied to all the previous questions. It is Jarvis Lorry who has alighted and stands with his hand on the coach door, replying to a group of officials. They leisurely walk round the carriage and leisurely mount the box, to look at what little luggage it carries on the roof; the country-people hanging about, press nearer to the coach doors and greedily stare in; a little child, carried by its mother, has its short arm held out for it, that it may touch the wife of an aristocrat who has gone to the guillotine.

"Behold your papers, Jarvis Lorry, countersigned."

"One can depart, citizen?"

"One can depart. Forward, my postillions! A good journey!"

"I salute you, citizens.—And the first danger passed!"

These are again the words of Jarvis Lorry, as he clasps his hands, and looks upward. There is terror in the carriage, there is weeping, there is the heavy breathing of the insensible traveller.

"Are we not going too slowly? Can they not be induced to go faster?" asks Lucie, clinging to the old man.

"It would seem like flight, my darling. I must not urge them too much; it would rouse suspicion."

"Look back, look back, and see if we are pursued!"

"The road is clear, my dearest. So far, we are not pursued."

Houses in twos and threes pass us by, solitary farms, ruinous buildings, dye-works, tanneries, and the like, open country, avenues of leafless trees. The hard, uneven pavement is under us, the soft, deep mud is on either side. Sometimes we strike into the skirting mud, to avoid the stones that clatter us and shake us; sometimes we stick in ruts and sloughs there. The agony of our impatience is then so great, that in our wild alarm and hurry we are for getting out and running—hiding —doing anything but stopping.

Out of the open country, in again among ruinous buildings, solitary farms, dye-works, tanneries, and the like, cottages in twos and threes, avenues of leafless trees. Have these men deceived us, and taken us back by another road? Is not this the same place twice over? Thank Heaven, no. A village. Look back, look back, and see if we are pursued! Hush! the posting-house.

Leisurely our four horses are taken out; leisurely the coach stands in the little street, bereft of horses, and with no likelihood upon it of ever moving again; leisurely the new horses come into visible existence, one by one; leisurely the new postillions follow, sucking and plaiting the lashes of their whips; leisurely the old postillions count their money, make wrong additions, and arrive at dissatisfied results. All the time, our over-fraught hearts are beating at a rate that would far outstrip the fastest gallop of the fastest horses ever foaled.

At length the new postillions are in their saddles, and the old are left behind. We are through the village, up the hill, and down the hill, and on the low watery grounds. Suddenly the postillions exchange speech with animated gesticulation, and the horses are pulled up, almost on their haunches. We are pursued!

" Ho! Within the carriage there. Speak then! "

" What is it? " asks Mr. Lorry, looking out at window.

" How many did they say? "

" I do not understand you."

" At the last post. How many to the guillotine to-day? "

" Fifty-two."

" I said so! A brave number! My fellow-citizen here, would have it forty-two; ten more heads are worth having. The guillotine goes handsomely. I love it. Hi forward. Whoop! "

The night comes on dark. He moves more; he is beginning to revive, and to speak intelligibly; he thinks they are still together; he asks him, by his name, what he has in his hand. O pity us, kind Heaven, and help us! Look out, look out, and see if we are pursued.

The wind is rushing after us, and the clouds are flying after us, and the moon is plunging after us, and the whole wild night is in pursuit of us; but, so far, we are pursued by nothing else.

CHARLES DICKENS—*A Tale of Two Cities.*

THROUGH THE ENEMY LINES

THE hero of this story is an old soldier of Napoleon's Guard, " Papa " Barlasch. In 1812, when the Emperor was preparing for his invasion of Russia, Barlasch came to Dantzig where he was billeted with Antoine Sebastian and his two daughters, Mathilde and Désirée. On his return from the Russian campaign he assists Désirée to escape from the city when it is besieged by the Russians. Rapp is the French general in command of the city. Louis d'Arragon is an officer on an English ship on service in the Baltic.

THROUGH THE ENEMY LINES

BARLASCH returned in the afternoon. He was leisurely and inclined to contemplativeness. It would seem that his preparations having all been completed, he was left with nothing to do. War is a purifier; it clears the social atmosphere and puts womanly men and manly women into their right places. It is also a simplifier; it teaches us to know how little we really require in daily life, and how many of the environments with which men and women hamper themselves are superfluous and the fruit of idleness.

"I have nothing to do," said Barlasch, "I will cook a careful dinner. All that I have saved in money I cannot carry away; all that was stored beneath the floor must be left there. It is often so in war."

He had told Désirée that they would have to walk twelve miles across the snow-clad marshes bordering the frozen Vistula, between midnight and dawn. It needed no telling that they could carry little with them.

"You will have to make a new beginning in life," he said curtly, "with the clothes upon your back. How many times have I done it—the Saints alone know! But take money, if you have it in gold or silver. Mine is all in copper gröschen, and it is too heavy to carry. I have never yet been anywhere that money was not useful—and name of a dog! I have never had it."

So Désirée divided what money she possessed with Barlasch, who added it carefully up and repeated several times for accuracy the tale of what he had received. For, like many who do not hesitate to steal, he was very particular in money matters.

"As for me," he said, "I shall make a new beginning, too. The Captain will enable me to get back to France, when I shall go to the Emperor again. It is no place for one of the Old Guard, here with Rapp. I am getting old, but he will find something for me to do, that little Emperor."

At midnight they set out, quitting the house in the Frauengasse noiselessly. The street was quiet enough, for half the houses were empty now. Their footsteps were inaudible on the trodden snow. It was a dark night and not cold; for the great frosts of this terrible winter were nearly over.

Barlasch carried his musket and bayonet. He had instructed Désirée to walk in front of him, should they meet a patrol. But Rapp had no men to spare for patrolling the town. There was no spirit left in Dantzig; for typhus and starvation patrolled the narrow streets.

They quitted the town to the north-west, near the Oliva Gate. There was no guard-house here because Langfuhr was held by the French, and Rapp's outposts were three miles out on the road to Zoppot.

"I have played this game for fifty years," said Barlasch, with a low laugh, when they reached the earthworks, completed, at such enormous cost of life and strength, by Rapp; "follow me and do as I do. When I stoop, stoop; when I crawl, crawl; when I run, run."

For he was a soldier now and nothing else. He stood erect, and looked round him with the air of a young man—ready, keen, alert. Then he moved forward with confidence towards the high land which terminates in the Johannesberg, where the peaceful Dantzigers now repair on a Sunday afternoon to drink thin beer and admire the view.

Below them on the right hand lay the marshes, a white expanse of snow with a single dark line drawn across it—the Langfuhr road with its double border of trees.

Barlasch turned once or twice to make sure that Désirée was following him; but he added nothing to his brief instructions. When he gained the summit of the tableland which runs parallel with the coast and the Langfuhr road, he paused for breath.

"When I crawl, crawl. When I run, run," he whispered again; and led the way. He went up the bed of a stream, turning his back to the coast, and at a certain point stopped and by a gesture of the hand bade Désirée crouch down and wait till he returned. He came back and signed to her to quit the bed of the stream and follow him. When she came up to the tableland, she found that they were quite close to a camp-fire. Through the low pines she could perceive the dark outline of a house.

"Now run," whispered Barlasch, leading the way across an open space which seemed to extend to the line of the horizon. Without looking back, Désirée ran—her only thought was a sudden surprise that Barlasch could move so quickly and silently.

When he gained the shelter of some trees, he threw

himself down on the snow, and Désirée, coming up to him, found him breathlessly holding his sides and laughing aloud.

"We are through the lines," he gasped, " name of a dog I was so frightened. There they go—pam! pam! Buz . . z . . z . ."

And he imitated the singing buzz of the bullets humming through the trees over their heads. For half a dozen shots were fired, while he was yet speaking, from behind the camp-fires. There were no more, however, and presently, having recovered his breath, Barlasch rose.

"Come," he said, " we have a long walk. *En route.*"

They made a great circuit in the pine-woods, through which Barlasch led the way with an unerring skill, and descending towards the plain far beyond Langfuhr they came out on to a lower tableland, below which the great marshes of the Vistula stretched in the darkness, slowly merging at last into the sea.

"Those," said Barlasch, pausing at the edge of the slope, " those are the lights of Oliva, where the Russians are. That line of lights straight in front is the Russian fleet lying off Zoppot, and with them are English ships. One of them is the little ship of Captain d'Arragon. And he will take you home with him; for the ship is ordered to England, to Plymouth—which is across the Channel from my own country. Ah—cristi! I sometimes want to see my own country again—and my own people—mademoiselle."

He went on a few paces and then stopped again, and in the darkness held up one hand, commanding silence. It was the churches of Dantzig striking the hour.

" Six o'clock," he whispered, " it will soon be dawn. Yes—we are half an hour too early."

He sat down, and, by a gesture, bade Désirée sit beside him.

" Yes," he said, " the Captain told me that he is bound for England to convoy larger ships, and you will sail in one of them. He has a home in the west of England, and he will take you there—a sister or a mother, I forget which—some woman. You cannot get on without women—you others. It is there that you will be happy, as the bon Dieu meant you to be. It is only in England that no one fears Napoleon. One may have a husband there and not fear that he will be killed. One may have children and not tremble for them—and it is that that makes you happy—you women."

Presently he rose and led the way down the slope. At the foot of it, he paused, and, pointing out a long line of trees, said in a whisper——

" He is there—where there are three taller trees. Between us and those trees are the French outposts. At dawn the Russians attack the outposts, and during the attack we have simply to go through it to those trees. There is no other way—that is the rendezvous. Those three tall trees. When I give the word, you get up and run to those trees—run without pausing, without looking round. I will follow. It is you he has come for—not Barlasch. You think I know nothing. Bah! I know everything. I have always known it—your poor little secret."

They lay on the snow, crouching in a ditch, until a grey line appeared low down in the Eastern sky and the horizon slowly distinguished itself from the thin thread of cloud that nearly always awaits the rising of the sun in Northern latitudes.

A minute later the dark group of trees broke into intermittent flame and the sharp, short "Hurrah!" of the Cossacks, like an angry bark, came sweeping across the plain on the morning breeze.

"Not yet," whispered Barlasch, with a gay chuckle of enjoyment. "Not yet—not yet. Listen, the bullets are not coming here, but are going past to the right of us. When you go, keep to the left. Slowly at first—keep a little breath till the end. Now, up! Mademoiselle, run; name of thunder, let us run!"

Désirée did not understand which were the French lines and which the line of Russian attack. But there was a clear way to the three trees which stood above the rest, and she went towards them. She knew she could not run so far, so she walked. Then the bullets, instead of passing to the right, seemed to play round her—like bees in a garden on a summer day—and she ran until she was tired.

The trees were quite close now, and the sky was light behind them. Then she saw Louis coming towards her, and she ran into his arms. The sound of the humming bullets was still in her dazed brain, and she touched him all over with her gloved hand as she clung to him, as a mother touches her child when it has fallen, to see whether it be hurt.

"How was I to know?" she whispered breathlessly. "How was I to know that you were to come into my life?"

The bullets did not matter, it seemed, nor the roar of

the firing to the right of them. Nothing mattered.

He held her and said nothing. And she wanted him to say nothing. Then she remembered Barlasch, and looked back over her shoulder.

" Where is Barlasch? " she asked, with a sudden sinking at her heart.

" He is coming slowly," replied Louis. " He came slowly behind you all the time, so as to draw the fire away from you."

They turned and waited for Barlasch, who seemed to be going in the wrong direction with an odd vagueness in his movements. Louis ran towards him with Désirée at his heels.

" Ça-y-est," said Barlasch; which cannot be translated, and yet has many meanings. " Ça-y-est."

And he sat down slowly on the snow. He sat quite upright and rigid, and in the cold light of the Baltic dawn they saw the meaning of his words. One hand was within his fur coat. He drew it out, and concealed it from Désirée behind his back. He did not seem to see them, but presently he put out his hand and lightly touched Désirée. Then he turned to Louis with that confidential drop of the voice with which he always distinguished his friends from those who were not his friends.

" What is she doing? " he asked. " I cannot see in the dark. Is it not dark? I thought it was. What is she doing? Saying a prayer? What—because I have my affair? Hey, mademoiselle. You may leave it to me. I will get in, I tell you that."

He put his finger to his nose, and then shook it from side to side with an air of deep cunning.

" Leave it to me. I shall slip in. Who will stop an old man, who has many wounds? Not St. Peter, assuredly. Let him try. And if the good God hears a commotion at the gate, He will only shrug His shoulders. He will say to St. Peter, 'Let pass; it is only Papa Barlasch!'"

And then there was silence. For Barlasch had gone to his own people.

H. SETON MERRIMAN—*Barlasch of the Guard.*

ADRIFT!

THE teller of this story is an apprentice sailor on board the barque *Florence* of Glasgow, and the place is somewhere off Cape Horn.

ADRIFT!

CAR-CONDUCTING may be the work of niceness and despatch, but it is ill training for working on the spars of a rolling ship. John Cutler was mousing clew-blocks on the main-yardarm, the ship lurched heavily, the foot-ropes were wet and slippery, and John, ill-balanced and unready, was cast into the sea. Instant, there was the cry " Man overboard "; the Old Man ordered the helm down, and, springing to the rack, threw a lifebuoy from the starboard quarter; the Second Mate, not seeing him throw it, threw another from the port.

We were below at the time, just after dinner, about to turn in, when we heard the call. All hands ran on deck. The watch were swinging the head yards; some were unlashing the lee boat. We joined them, tore the cover off, hooked the tackles, and swung her out. There was confusion; the Old Man and the Mate shouting cross orders, the boat swinging wildly on the tackles, men crowding about the rail.

" Another hand in the boat," yelled the Second Mate, as he sprang into the stern-sheets, " lower away, you! "

There was a whirr of block sheaves, the falls smoking on the pins, a splash, a rush of water on the rusty side. " Bow off, there! Bow off, you! " and I found myself in the bow of the boat, tugging frantically at the heft of a long oar.

There was that in the steady *clack—clack-a* of oar on rowlock to soothe the tremors of our moment of excited haste. Astern was the barque, her mainyards aback, rolling heavily athwart the swell; we were leaving her slowly, for, though the breeze was light, we had to climb the long steep slopes of a Cape Horn swell. Old Martin's broad back was bent to the oar in front of me, Houston beyond, and the bo'sun at the stroke. The Second Mate was standing up at the tiller, listening for a hail, gazing anxiously ahead for gleam of a painted lifebuoy. *Clack—clack-a, clack—clack-a*; the bo'sun was setting us a feverish stroke; it couldn't last. *Clack—clack-a, clack—clack-a*; we were already breathing heavily. Up and down the heaving swell we went; crawling laboured to the crown—the shudder, and the quick, sickening descent! *Clack—clack-a!* Would it ever end? Now I was pulling out of stroke—a feeble paddle. My neck! I had the pain there! . . . "Bow, there! Lay in, an' keep yer eyes about. He must be here somewhere!"

I laid in my oar, and faced about. We could not see far, the swell was too great. When the boat rose we had a hasty glimpse of the face of the water, but in the hollow, the great glassy walls rose ahead and astern. We thought we had overrun the distance, and lay-to for a time. Then on again, shouting as we went. The Second Mate saw something on the crest of a roller, just a glimpse, and we pulled to it. It was Cutler's round cap; we had steered a good course. Near by we found him with his arm twisted round the grab rope of the lifebuoy. He was dazed and quiet when we dragged him over the stern.

We were about to return when Mr. M'Kellar thought of the second lifebuoy.

"Bow, there! D'ye see the other buoy; it'll be somewhere t' th' norrard!"

I stood up, unsteadily. There was something white in the hollow of a farther roller. We edged over; it was but a fleck of foam. Farther over, up and down the swell we climbed until we found it. We turned to row back. "Back starboard! Pull port, you!" the boat's head swung round, and we rose quickly on the following swell.

There was a startled cry from the stern-sheets, "*O Dhia! O Dhia!*"

Well might M'Kellar cry out, for, unobserved of any, the mist had closed in on us. There was no ship in sight, no point to steer for—nothing to guide, there was only the great glassy walls rising and falling, moving up into the thickening mist.

A panic seized us; furiously we rowed, driving the boat into it with no thought of course or distance. She was awash underfoot before we exhausted ourselves, and lay, breathing heavily, over the oars.

The bo'sun was the first to regain a state of sanity. "Vast rowin'," he cried; "vast rowin'! We cawn't do no good like this. Liy 'er to, Mister! Liy-to; it's the ownly thing."

M'Kellar put the tiller over, and we brought her head to swell again.

We stood up, all eyes a-watching; we shouted together, listened intent; there was no friendly sail looming in the mist, no answer to our cries. We rowed aimlessly. Sometimes we fancied we could hear a hail or a creak of blocks. We would lash blindly at the oars till the foam flew, then lie-to again. There was no compass in the boat, no food; only a small barreca of water. Sometimes it is thick weather off the Horn for days! If the mist held?

Cutler, crouching, shivering in the stern-sheets, began to cry like a child. Cold, wet, unnerved, he was feeling worst of us all. "Shut up," said the Second Mate, dragging off his jacket and throwing it over the shivering lad. Old Martin was strangely quiet; he, too, was shivering. He had been just about to turn in when he heard the call, and was ill-clad for boat service. Only once did he show a bit of his old gallant truculence.

"All right, Mister! If we loses track o' th' ship, we've got plenty o' provisions! We can eat them lifebuoys, wot ye was so keen a-gettin'!"

"Oh, quit yer chinnin', ye old croak! Oo's talkin' abaht losin' track o' th' ship!" The bo'sun didn't like to think! Cutler became light-headed, and began to talk wildly; he would stand up, pointing and shouting out, "There she is, there!" Then he began to make queer noises, and became very quiet. There was the canvas boat cover lying in the bottom of the boat. The bo'sun put this round him, and I was ordered aft to rub him down.

The cold became intense. When the heat of our mad spurt had passed, depression came on us and we cowered, chilled to the marrow by the mist, on the gratings of the heaving boat. Long we lay thus, Houston and the bo'sun pulled a listless stroke to keep her head to the swell. We had no count of time. Hours must have passed, we thought.

"The Dago 'll hae ma trick at th' wheel, noo," said Houston strangely. "It was ma turn at fower bells!"

No one heeded him.

"They'll hae tae shift some o' th' hauns i' th' watches, eh? . . . wi' you, an' Martin, an' th' young fla' no' there!" he continued.

"Oh, shut up! Shut up, an' listen. *O Dhia!* can ye hear nocht?" M'Kellar, standing up on the stern-sheets, was casting wild glances into the pall that enshrouded us. "Here! All together, men—a shout!"

A weakly chorus went out over the water.

Silence.

Suddenly Houston stood up. "Maister, did ye hear that—a cheep!" We thought that he was going off like Cutler; we could hear nothing. "A cheep, Ah telt ye, Maister; a cheep, as shair's daith!" Houston was positive. "The jerk o' a rudder, or" . . . Almost on top of us there was a flash of blinding fire, the roar of a gun followed!

We sprang to the oars, shouting madly—shaping out of the mist was the loom of a square sail, there was sound of a bell struck. No need now to talk of eating lifebuoys; Houston would be in time for his trick at the wheel!

.   .   .   .

"What kept ye, Mister? We saw ye pickin' th' man up! What made ye turn t' th' norrard?" The Old Man had a note of anger in his voice.

"Well, Sir, we couldn't see th' other buoy, an' I thought it a peety if we didn't pick it up; an' while we were lookin' for it, we lost track o' th' ship," said Mister M'Kellar, ashamed and miserable.

The Mate broke in, "Fool! D'ye mean t' tell us ye risked a whole boat's crew for a tuppence-ha'penny lifebuoy? B'gad, it would serve ye right if ye had t' go seekin' like th' Flying Dutchman!" The Mate continued to curse such stupidity, but the Old Man, though permitting the Mate to rail, was wonderfully silent. After all, M'Kellar, like himself, was a Scotchman, and much may be forgiven to a Scotchman—looking after his owner's property!

D. W. BONE—*The Brassbounder.*

A BRAVE DECISION

IT is France on the evening of the 4th of August, 1789.
Adrien du Pont, Vicomte de Saux, who in childhood was
betrothed to Mademoiselle Denise de St. Alais, is telling the
story.

A BRAVE DECISION

At that time a brazier in the market-place, and three or four lanterns at street crossings, made up the most of the public lighting. When I paused, therefore, to breathe my horse on the brow of the slope, beyond the Valandré bridge, and looked back on Cahors, I saw only darkness, broken here and there by a blur of yellow light; that still, by throwing up a fragment of wall or eaves, told in a mysterious way of the sleeping city.

The river, a faint, shimmering line, conjectured rather than seen, wound round all. Above, clouds were flying across the sky, and a wind, cold for the time of year—cold, at least, after the heat of the day—chilled the blood, and slowly filled the mind with the solemnity of night.

As I stood listening to the breathing of the horses, the excitement in which I had passed the last few hours died away, and left me wondering—wondering, and a little regretful. The exaltation gone, I found the scene I had just left flavourless; I even presently began to find it worse. Some false note in the cynical, boastful voices and the selfish—the utterly selfish—plans, to which I had been listening for hours, made itself heard in the stillness. Madame's " We are France," which had sounded well amid the lights and glitter of the *salon*, among lace and *fripons* and rose-pink coats, seemed folly in the face of the infinite night, behind which lay twenty-five million of Frenchmen.

However, what I had done, I had done. I had the white cockade on my breast; I was pledged to order—and to my order. And it might be the better course. But, with reflection, enthusiasm faded; and, by some strange process, as it faded, and the scene in which I had just taken part lost its hold, the errand that had brought me to Cahors recovered importance. As Madame St. Alais' influence grew weak, the memory of Mademoiselle, sitting lonely and scared in her coach, grew vivid, until I turned my horse fretfully, and endeavoured to lose the thought in rapid movement.

But it is not so easy to escape from oneself at night, as in the day. The soughing of the wind through the chestnut trees, the drifting clouds, and the sharp ring of hoofs on the road, all laid as it were a solemn finger on the pulses and stilled them. The men behind me talked in sleepy voices, or rode silently. The town lay a hundred leagues behind. Not a light appeared on the upland. In the world of night through which we rode, a world of black, mysterious hulks rising suddenly against the grey sky, and as suddenly sinking, we were the only inhabitants.

At last we reached the hill above St. Alais, and I looked eagerly for lights in the valley; forgetting that, as it wanted only an hour of midnight, the village would have retired hours before. The disappointment, and the delay—for the steepness of the hill forbade any but a walking pace—fretted me; and when I heard, a moment later, a certain noise behind me, a noise I knew only too well, I flared up.

"Stay, fool!" I cried, reining in my horse, and turning in the saddle. "That mare has broken her shoe again, and you are riding on as if nothing were the matter. Get down and see. Do you think that I——"

"Pardon, Monsieur," Gil muttered. He had been sleeping in his saddle.

He scrambled down. The mare he rode, a valuable one, had a knack of breaking her hind shoe; after which she never failed to lame herself at the first opportunity. Buton had tried every method of shoeing, but without success.

I sprang to the ground while he lifted the foot. My ear had not deceived me; the shoe was broken. Gil tried to remove the jagged fragment left on the hoof, but the mare was restive, and he had to desist.

"She cannot go to Saux in that state," I cried angrily.

The men were silent for a moment, peering at the mare. Then Gil spoke.

"The St. Alais forge is not three hundred yards down the lane, Monsieur," he said. "And the turn is yonder. We could knock up Petit Jean, and get him to bring his pincers here. Only——"

"Only what?" I said peevishly.

"I quarrelled with him at Cahors Fair, Monsieur," Gil answered sheepishly; "and he might not come for us."

"Very well," I said gruffly, "I will go. And do you stay here, and keep the mare quiet."

André held the stirrup for me to mount. The smithy, the first hovel in the village, was a quarter of a mile away, and, in reason, I should have ridden to it. But, in my irritation, I was ready to do anything they did not propose, and roughly rejecting his help, I started on foot. Fifty paces brought me to the branch road that led to St. Alais, and making out the turning with a little difficulty, I plunged into it; losing, in a moment, the cheerful sound of jingling bits and the murmur of the men's voices.

Poplars rose on high banks on either side of the lane, and made the place as dark as a pit, and I had almost to grope my way. A stumble added to my irritation, and I cursed the St. Alais for the ruts, and the moon for its untimely setting. The ceaseless whispering of the poplar leaves went with me, and, in some unaccountable way, annoyed me. I stumbled again, and swore at Gil, and then stopped to listen. I was in the road, and yet I heard the jingling of bits again, as if the horses were following me.

I stopped angrily to listen, thinking that the men had disobeyed my orders. Then I found that the sound came from the front, and was heavier and harder than the ringing of bit or bridle. I groped my way forward, wondering somewhat, until a faint, ruddy light, shining on the darkness and the poplars, prepared me for the truth—welcome, though it seemed of the strangest— that the forge was at work.

As I took this in, I turned a corner, and came within sight of the smithy; and stood in astonishment. The forge was in full blast. Two hammers were at work; I could see them rising and falling, and hear, though they seemed to be muffled, the rhythmical jarring clang as they struck the metal. The ruddy glare of the fire flooded the road and burnished the opposite trees, and flung long, black shadows on the sky.

Such a sight filled me with the utmost astonishment for it was nearly midnight. Fortunately, something else I saw astonished me still more, and stayed my foot Between the point where I stood by the hedge and the forge a number of men were moving, and flitting to and fro; men with bare arms and matted heads, half-naked, with skins burned black. It would have been hard to count them, they shifted so quickly; and I did not try. It was enough for me that one half of them carried pikes and pitchforks, that one man seemed to be detailing them into groups, and giving them directions; and that, notwithstanding the occasional jar of the hammers, an air of ferocious stealth marked their movements.

For a moment I stood rooted to the spot. Then, instinctively, I stepped aside into the shadow of the hedge, and looked again. The man who acted as the leader carried an axe on his shoulder, the broad blade of which, as it caught the glow of the furnace, seemed to be bathed in blood. He was never still—this man. One moment he moved from group to group, gesticulating, ordering, encouraging. Now he pulled a man out of one troop and thrust him forcibly into another; now he made a little speech, which was dumb play to me, a hundred paces away; now he went into the forge, and his huge bulk for a moment intercepted the light. It was Petit Jean, the smith.

I made use of the momentary darkness which he caused on one of these occasions, and stole a little nearer. For I knew now what was before me. I knew perfectly that all this meant blood, fire, outrage, flames rising to heaven, screams startling the stricken night. But I must know more, if I would do anything. I went nearer, therefore, creeping along the hedge, and crouching in the ditch, until no more than twelve yards separated me from the muster. Then I stood still, as Petit Jean came out again to distribute another bundle of weapons, clutched instantly and eagerly by grimy hands. I could hear now, and I shuddered at what I heard. Gargouf was in every mouth. Gargouf, the St. Alais' steward, coupled with grisly tortures and slow deaths, with old sins, and outrages, and tyrannies, now for the first time voiced, now to be expiated!

At last, one man laid the torch by crying aloud, " To the Château! To the Château! " and in an instant the words changed the feelings with which I had hitherto stared into immediate horror. I started forward. My impulse, for a moment, was to step into the light and confront them—to persuade, menace, cajole, turn them any way from their purpose. But in the same moment, reflection showed me the hopelessness of the attempt. These were no longer peasants, dull, patient clods, such as I had known all my life; but maddened beasts; I read it in their gestures and the growl of their voices. To step forward would be only to sacrifice myself; and with this thought I crept back, gained the deeper shadow, and, turning on my heel, sped down the lane. The ruts and the darkness were no longer anything to me. If I stumbled, I did not notice it. If I fell, it was no matter. In less than a minute I was standing, breathless, by the astonished servants, striving to tell them quickly what they must do.

"The village is rising!" I panted. "They are going to burn the Château, and Mademoiselle is in it! Gil, ride, gallop, lose not a minute, to Cahors, and tell M. le Marquis. He must bring what forces he can. And do you, André, go to Saux. Tell Father Benôit. Bid him do his utmost—bring all he can."

For answer, they stared, open-mouthed, through the dusk. "And the mare, Monsieur?" one asked at last dully.

"Fool! let her go!" I cried. "The mare? Do you understand? The Château is——"

"And you, Monsieur?"

"I am going to the house by the garden wing. Now go! Go, men!" I continued. "A hundred livres to each of you if the house is saved!"

I said the house, because I dared not speak what was really in my mind; because I dared not picture the girl, young, helpless, a woman, in the hands of those monsters. Yet it was that which goaded me now, it was that which gave me such strength that, before the men had ridden many yards, I had forced my way through the thick fence, as if it had been a mass of cobwebs. Once on the other side, in the open, I hastened across one field and a second, skirted the village, and made for the gardens which abutted on the east wing of the Château. I knew these well; the part farthest from the house, and most easy of entrance, was a wilderness, in which I had often played as a child. There was no fence round this, except a wooden paling, and none between it and the more orderly portion; while a side door opened from the latter into a passage leading to the great hall of the Château. The house, a long, regular building, reared by the Marquis's father, was composed of two wings and a main block. All faced the end of the village street at a distance of a hundred paces; a wide, dusty, ill-planted avenue leading from the iron gates, which stood always open, to the state entrance.

The rioters had only a short distance to go, therefore, and no obstacle between them and the house; none when they reached it of greater consequence than ordinary doors and shutters, should the latter be closed. As I ran, I shuddered to think how defenceless all lay; and how quickly the wretches, bursting in the doors, would overrun the shining parquets, and sweep up the spacious staircase.

The thought added wings to my feet. I had farther to go than they had, and over hedges, but before the first sounds of their approach reached the house I was already in the wilderness, and forcing my way through it, stumbling over stumps and bushes, falling more than once, covered with dust and sweat, but still pushing on.

At last I sprang into the open garden, with its shadowy walks, and nymphs, and fauns; and looked towards the village. A dull red light was beginning to show among the trunks of the avenue; a murmur of voices sounded in the distance. They were coming! I wasted no more than a single glance; then I ran down the walk, between the statues. In a moment I passed into the darker shadow under the house, I was at the door. I thrust my shoulder against it. It resisted; it resisted! and every moment was precious. I could no longer see the approaching lights nor hear the voices of the crowd—the angle of the house intervened; but I could imagine only too vividly how they were coming on; I fancied them already at the great door.

I hammered on the panels with my fist; then I fumbled for the latch, and found it. It rose, but the door held. I shook it. I shook it again in a frenzy at last, forgetting caution, I shouted—shouted more loudly. Then, after an age, as it seemed to me standing panting in the darkness, I heard halting foot steps come along the passage, and saw a line of light grow, and brighten under the door. At last a quaver ing voice asked:—

"Who is it?"

"M. de Saux," I answered impatiently. "M. de Saux! Let me in. Let me in, do you hear?" And I struck the panels wrathfully.

"Monsieur," the voice answered, quavering more and more, "is there anything the matter?"

"Matter? They are going to burn the house, fool!" I cried. "Open! open! if you do not wish to be burned in your beds!"

For a moment I fancied that the man still hesitated. Then he unbarred. In a twinkling I was inside, in a narrow passage, with dingy, stained walls. An old man, lean-jawed and feeble, an old valet whom I had often seen at worsted work in the ante-room, confronted me, holding an iron candlestick. The light shook in his hands, and his jaw fell as he looked at me. I saw that I had nothing to expect from him, and I snatched the bar from his hands, and set it back in its place myself. Then I seized the light.

"Quick!" I said passionately. "To your mistress."

"Monsieur?"

"Upstairs! Upstairs!"

He had more to say, but I did not wait to hear it. Knowing the way, and having the candle, I left him, and hurried along the passage. Stumbling over three or four mattresses that lay on the floor, doubtless for the servants, I reached the hall. Here my taper shone a mere speck in a cavern of blackness; but it gave me light enough to see that the door was barred, and I turned to the staircase. As I set my foot on the lowest step the old valet, who was following me as fast as his trembling legs would carry him, blundered against a spinning-wheel that stood in the hall. It fell with a clatter, and in a moment a chorus of screams and cries broke out above. I sprang up the stairs three at a stride, and in the lobby came on the screamers—a terrified group, whose alarm the doubtful light of a tallow candle, that stood beside them on the floor, could not exaggerate. Nearest to me stood an old footman and a boy—their terror-stricken eyes met mine as I mounted the last stairs. Behind them, and crouching against a tapestry-covered seat that ran along the wall, were the rest; three or four women, who shrieked and hid their faces in one another's garments. They did not look up or take any heed of me; but continued to scream steadily.

The old man with a quavering oath tried to still them.

"Where is Gargouf?" I asked him.

"He has gone to fasten the back doors, Monsieur," he answered.

"And Mademoiselle?"

"She is yonder."

He turned as he spoke; and I saw behind him a heavy curtain hiding the oriel window of the lobby. It moved while I looked, and Mademoiselle emerged from its folds, her small, childish face pale, but strangely composed. She wore a light, loose robe, hastily arranged, and had her hair hanging free at her back. In the gloom and confusion, which the feeble candle did little to disperse, she did not at first see me.

" Has Gargouf come back? " she asked.

" No, Mademoiselle, but——"

The man was going to point me out; she interrupted him with a sharp cry of anger.

" Stop these fools," she said. " Oh, stop these fools! I cannot hear myself speak. Let someone call Gargouf! Is there no one to do anything? "

One of the old men pottered off to do it, leaving her standing in the middle of the terror-stricken group; a white pathetic little figure, keeping fear at bay with both hands. The dark curtains behind threw her face and form into high relief; but admiration was the last thought in my mind.

" Mademoiselle," I said, " you must fly by the garden door."

She started and stared at me, her eyes dilating.

" Monsieur de Saux," she muttered. " Are you here? I do not—I do not understand. I thought——"

" The village is rising," I said. " In a moment they will be here."

" They are here already," she answered faintly.

She meant only that she had seen their approach from the window; but a dull murmur that at the moment rose on the air outside, and penetrating the walls, grew

128

each instant louder and more sinister, seemed to give another significance to her words. The women listened with white faces, then began to scream afresh. A reckless movement of one of them dashed out the nearer of the two lights. The old man who had admitted me began to whimper.

"*O mon Dieu!*" I cried fiercely, "can no one still these cravens?" For the noise almost robbed me of the power of thought, and never had thought been more necessary. "Be still, fools," I continued, "no one will hurt *you*. And do you, Mademoiselle, please to come with me. There is not a moment to be lost. The garden by which I entered——"

But she looked at me in such a way that I stopped.

"Is it necessary to go?" she said doubtfully. "Is there no other way, Monsieur?"

The noise outside was growing louder. "What men have you?" I said.

"Here is Gargouf," she answered promptly. "He will tell you."

I turned to the staircase and saw the steward's face, at all times harsh and grim, rising out of the well of the stairs. He had a candle in one hand and a pistol in the other; and his features as his eyes met mine wore an expression of dogged anger, the sight of which drew fresh cries from the women. But I rejoiced to see him, for he at least betrayed no signs of flinching. I asked him what men he had.

"You see them," he answered drily, betraying no surprise at my presence.

"Only these?"

"There were three more," he said. "But I found the

doors unbarred, and the men gone. I am keeping this," he continued, with a dark glance at his pistol, " for one of them."

" Mademoiselle must go! " I said.

He shrugged his shoulders with an indifference that maddened me. " How? " he asked.

" By the garden door."

" They are there. The house is surrounded."

I cried out at that in despair; and on the instant, as if to give point to his words, a furious blow fell on the great doors below, and awakening every echo in the house, proclaimed that the moment was come. A second shock followed; then a rain of blows. While the maids shrieked and clung to one another, I looked at Mademoiselle, and she at me.

" We must hide you," I muttered.

" No," she said.

" There must be some place," I said, looking round me desperately, and disregarding her answer. The noise of the blows was deafening. " In the——"

" I will not hide, Monsieur," she answered. Her cheeks were white, and her eyes seemed to flicker with each blow. But the maiden who had been dumb before me a few days earlier was gone; in her place I saw Mademoiselle de St. Alais, conscious of a hundred ancestors. " They are our people. I will meet them," she continued, stepping forward bravely, though her lip trembled. " Then if they dare——"

" They are mad," I answered. " They are mad! Yet it is a chance; and we have few! If I can get to them before they break in, I may do something. One moment, Mademoiselle; screen the light, will you? "

Someone did so, and I turned feverishly and caught hold of the curtain. But Gargouf was before me. He seized my arm, and for the moment checked me.

"What is it? What are you going to do?" he growled.

"Speak to them from the window."

"They will not listen."

"Still I will try. What else is there?"

"Lead and iron," he answered in a tone that made me shiver. "Here are M. le Marquis's sporting guns; they shoot straight. Take one, M. le Vicomte; I will take the other. There are two more, and the men can shoot. We can hold the staircase, at least."

I took one of the guns mechanically, amid a dismal uproar; wailing and the thunder of blows within, outside the savage booing of the crowd. No help could come for another hour; and for a moment in this desperate strait my heart failed me. I wondered at the steward's courage.

"You are not afraid?" I said. I knew how he had trampled on the poor wretches outside; how he had starved them and ground them down, and misused them through long years.

He cursed the dogs.

"You will stand by Mademoiselle?" I said feverishly. I think it was to hearten myself by his assurance.

He squeezed my hand in a grip of iron, and I asked no more. In a moment, however, I cried aloud.

"Ah, but they will burn the house!" I said. "What is the use of holding the staircase, when they can burn us like rats?"

"We shall die together," was his only answer. And he kicked one of the weeping, crouching women. "Be still, you whelp!" he said. "Do you think that will help you?"

But I heard the door below groan, and I sprang to the window and dragged aside the curtain, letting in a ruddy glow that dyed the ceiling the colour of blood. My one fear was that I might be too late; that the door would yield or the crowd break in at the back before I could get a hearing. Luckily, the casement gave to the hand, and I thrust it open, and, meeting a cold blast of air, in a twinkling was outside, on the narrow ledge of the window over the great doors, looking down on such a scene as few châteaux in France had witnessed since the days of the third Henry—God be thanked!

A little to one side the great dovecot was burning, and sending up a trail of smoke that, blown across the avenue, hid all beyond in a murky reek, through which the flames now and again flickered hotly. Men, busy as devils, black against the light, were plying the fire with straw. Beyond the dovecot, an outhouse and a stack were blazing; and nearer, immediately before the house, a crowd of moving figures were hurrying to and fro, some battering the doors and windows, others bringing fuel, all moving, yelling, laughing—laughing the laughter of fiends to the music of crackling flames and shivering glass.

I saw Petit Jean in the forefront giving orders; and men round him. There were women, too, hanging on the skirts of the men; and one woman, in the midst of all, half-naked, screaming curses, and brandishing her arms. It was she who added the last touch of horror to the scene; and she, too, who saw me first, and pointed me out with dreadful words, and cursed me, and the house, and cried for our blood.

Some called for silence, while others stared at me stupidly, or pointed me out to their fellows; but the greater part took up the woman's cry, and, enraged by my presence, shook their fists at me, and shouted vile threats and viler abuse. For a minute the air rang with " *A bas les Seigneurs! A bas les tyrans!* " And I found this bad enough. But, presently, whether they caught sight of the steward, or merely returned to their first hatred, from which my appearance had only for the moment diverted them, the cry changed to a sullen roar of " Gargouf! Gargouf! " A roar so full of the lust for blood, and coupled with threats so terrible, that the heart sickened and the cheek grew pale at the sound.

" Gargouf! Gargouf! Give us Gargouf! " they howled. " Give us Gargouf! and he shall eat hot gold! Give us Gargouf, and he shall need no more of our daughters! "

I shuddered to think that Mademoiselle heard; shuddered to think of the peril in which she stood. The wretches below were no longer men; under the influence of this frenzied woman they were mad brute beasts, drunk with fire and licence. As the smoke from the burning building eddied away for a moment across the crowd and hid it, and still that hoarse cry came out of the mirk, I could believe that I heard not men, but maddened hounds raving in the kennel.

Again the smoke drifted away; and someone in

the rear shot at me. I heard the glass splinter beside me. Another, a little nearer, flung up a burning fragment that, alighting on the ledge, blazed and spluttered by my foot. I kicked it down.

The act, for a moment, stilled the riot, and I seized the opportunity. "You dogs!" I said, striving to make my voice heard above the hissing of the flames. "Begone! The soldiers from Cahors are on the road. I sent for them this hour back. Begone before they come, and I will intercede for you. Stay and do further mischief, and you shall hang, to the last man!"

Some answered with a yell of derision, crying out that the soldiers were with them. More, that the nobles were abolished, and their houses given to the people. One, who was drunk, kept shouting, "*A bas la Bastille! A bas la Bastille!*" with a stupid persistence.

A moment more and I should lose my chance. I waved my hand! "What do you want?" I cried.

"Justice!" one shouted, and another, "Vengeance!" A third, "Gargouf!" And then all, "Gargouf! Gargouf!" until Petit Jean stilled the tumult.

"Have done!" he cried to them, in his coarse, brutal voice. "Have we come here only to yell? And do you, Seigneur, give up Gargouf, and you shall go free. Otherwise, we will burn the house, and all in it."

"You villain!" I said. "We have guns, and——"

"The rats have teeth, but they burn! They burn!" he answered, pointing triumphantly, with the axe he held, to the flaming buildings. "They burn! Yet listen, Seigneur," he continued, "and you shall have a minute to make up your minds. Give up Gargouf to us to do with as we please, and the rest shall go."

" All? "

" All."

I trembled. " But Gargouf, man? " I said. " Will you—what will you do with him? "

" Roast him! " the smith cried, with a fearful oath; and the wretches round him laughed like fiends. " Roast him, when we have plucked him bare."

I shuddered. From Cahors help could not come for another hour. From Saux it might not come at all. The doors below me could not stand long, and these brutes were thirty to one, and mad with the lust of vengeance. With the wrongs, the crimes, the vices of centuries to avenge, they dreamed that the day of requital was come; and the dream had turned clods into devils. The very flames they had kindled gave them assurance of it. The fire was in their blood. *A bas la Bastille! A bas les tyrans!*

I hesitated.

" One minute! " the smith cried, with a boastful gesture—" one minute we give you! Gargouf or all."

" Wait! "

I turned and went in—turned from the smoky glare, the circling pigeons, the grotesque black figures, and the terror and confusion of the night, and went in to that other scene scarcely less dreadful to me; though only two candles, guttering in tin sockets, lit the landing, and it borrowed from the outside no more than the ruddy reflection of horror. The women had ceased to scream and sob, and crowded together silent and panic-stricken. The old men and the lad moistened their lips, and looked furtively from the arms they handled to one another's faces. Mademoiselle alone stood erect, pale, firm. I shot a glance at the slender little figure in the white robe, then I looked away. I dared not say what I had in my mind. I knew that she had heard, and——

She said it! " You have answered them? " she muttered, her eyes meeting mine.

" No," I said, looking away again. " They have given us a minute to decide, and——"

" I heard them," she answered, shivering. " Tell them."

" But, Mademoiselle——"

" Tell them never! Never! " she cried feverishly. " Be quick, or they will think that we are dreaming of it."

Yet I hesitated—while the flames crackled outside. What, after all, was this rascal's life beside hers? What his tainted existence, who all these years had ground the faces of the poor and dishonoured the helpless, beside her youth? It was a dreadful moment, and I hesitated. " Mademoiselle," I muttered at last, avoiding her eyes, " you have not thought, perhaps. But to refuse this offer may be to sacrifice all—and not save him."

" I have thought! " she answered, with a passionate gesture. " I have thought. But he was my father's steward, Monsieur, and he is my brother's; if he has sinned, it was for them. It is for them to pay the penalty. And—after all, it may not come to that," she continued, her face changing, and her eyes seeking mine, full of sudden terror. " They will not dare, I think. They will never dare to——"

" Where is he? " I asked hoarsely.

She pointed to the corner behind her. I looked, and

could scarcely believe my eyes. The man whom I had left full of a desperate courage, prepared to sell his life dearly, now crouched a huddled figure in the darkest angle of the tapestry seat. Though I had spoken of him in a low voice, and without naming him, he heard me, and looked up, and showed a face to match his attitude; a face pallid and sweating with fear; a face that, vile at the best and when redeemed by hardihood, looked now the vilest thing on earth. *Ciel!* that fear should reduce man to that! He tried to speak as his eyes met mine, but his lips moved inaudibly, and he only crouched lower, the picture of panic and guilt.

I cried out to the others to know what had happened to him. "What is it?" I said.

No one answered; and then I seemed to know. While he had thought all in danger, while he had felt himself only one among many, the common courage of a man had supported him. But God knows what voices, only too well known to him, what accents of starving men and wronged women, had spoken in that fierce cry for his life! What plaints from the dead, what curses of babes hanging on dry breasts! At any rate, whatever he had heard in that call for his blood, *his* blood—it had unmanned him. In a moment, in a twinkling, it had dashed him back into his corner, a trembling craven, holding up his hands for his life.

Such fear is infectious, and I strode to him in a rage and shook him.

"Get up, hound!" I said. "Get up and strike a blow for your life; or, by heaven, no one else will!"

He stood up. "Yes, yes, Monsieur," he muttered. "I will! I will stand up for Mademoiselle. I will——"

But I heard his teeth chatter, and I saw that his eyes wandered this way and that, as do a hare's when the dogs close on it; and I knew that I had nothing to expect from him. A howl outside warned me at the same moment that our respite was spent; and I flung him off and turned to the window.

Too late, however; before I could reach it, a thundering blow on the doors below set the candles flickering and the women shrieking; then for an instant I thought that all was over. A stone came through the window; another followed it, and another. The shattered glass fell over us; the draught put out one light, and the women, terrified beyond control, ran this way and that with the other, shrieking dismally. This, the yelling of the crowd outside, the sombre light and more sombre glare, the utter confusion and panic, so distracted me, that for a moment I stood irresolute, inactive, looking wildly about me; a poltroon waiting for someone to lead. Then a touch fell on my arm, and I turned and found Mademoiselle at my side, and saw her face upturned to mine.

It was white, and her eyes were wide with the terror she had so long repressed. Her hold on me grew heavier; she swayed against me, clinging to me.

"Oh!" she whispered in my ear in a voice that went to my heart. "Save me! Save me! Can nothing be done? Can nothing be done, Monsieur? Must we die?"

"We must gain time," I said. My courage returned wonderfully, as I felt her weight on my arm. "All is not over yet," I said. "I will speak to them."

And setting her on the seat, I sprang to the window

138

and passed through it. Outside, things at a first glance seemed unchanged. The wavering flames, the glow, the trail of smoke and sparks, all were there. But a second glance showed that the rioters no longer moved to and fro about the fire, but were massed directly below me in a dense body round the doors, waiting for them to give way. I shouted to them frantically, hoping still to delay them. I called Petit Jean by name. But I could not make myself heard in the uproar, or they would not heed; and while I vainly tried, the great doors yielded at last, and with a roar of triumph the crowd burst in.

Not a moment was to be lost. I sprang back through the window, clutching up as I did so the gun Gargouf had given me; and then I stood in amazement. The landing was empty! The rush of feet across the hall below shook the house. Ten seconds and the mob, whose screams of triumph already echoed through the passages, would be on us. But where was Mademoiselle? Where was Gargouf? Where were the servants, the waiting-maids, the boy, whom I had left here?

I stood an instant paralysed, like a man in a nightmare; brought up short in that supreme moment. Then, as the first crash of heavy feet sounded on the stairs, I heard a faint scream, somewhere to my right, as I stood. On the instant I sprang to the door which, on that side, led to the left wing. I tore it open and passed through it—not a moment too soon. The slightest delay, and the foremost rioters must have seen me. As it was I had time to turn the key, which, fortunately, was on the inside.

Then I hurried across the room, making my way to

an open door at the farther end, from which light issued; I passed through the room beyond, which was empty, then into the last of the suite.

Here I found the fugitives; who had fled, so precipitately that they had not even thought of closing the doors behind them. In this last refuge—Madame's boudoir, all white and gold—I found them crouching among gilt-backed chairs and flowered cushions. They had brought only one candle with them; and the silks and gew-gaws and knick-knacks on which its light shone dimly, gave a peculiar horror to their white faces and glaring eyes, as, almost mad with terror, they huddled in the farthest corner and stared at me.

They were such cowards that they put Mademoiselle foremost; or it was she who stood out to meet me. She knew me before they did, therefore, and quieted them. When I could hear my own voice, I asked where Gargouf was.

They had not discovered that he was not with them, and they cried out, saying that he had come that way.

" You followed him? "

" Yes, Monsieur."

This explained their flight, but not the steward's absence. What matter where he had gone, however, since his help could avail little. I looked round—looked round in despair; the very simpering Cupids on the walls seemed to mock our danger. I had the gun, I could fire one shot, I had one life in my hands. But to what end? In a moment, at any moment, within a minute or two at most, the doors would be forced and the horde of mad brutes would pour in upon us and——

" Ah, Monsieur, the closet staircase! He has gone by the closet staircase! "

It was the boy who spoke. He alone of them had his wits about him.

" Where is it? " I said.

The lad sprang forward to show me, but Mademoiselle was before him with the candle. She flew back into the passage, a passage of four or five feet only between that room and the second of the suite; in the wall of this she flung open a door, apparently of a closet. I looked in and saw the beginning of a staircase. My heart leaped at the sight.

" To the floor above? " I said.

" No, Monsieur, to the roof! "

" Up, up, then! " I cried in a frenzy of impatience. " It will give us time. Quick. They are coming."

For I heard the door at the end of the suite, the door I had locked, creak and yield. They were forcing it, at any moment it might give; where I stood waiting to bring up the rear their hoarse cries and curses came to my ears. But the good door held; it held, long enough at any rate. Before it gave way we were on the stairs and I had shut the door of the closet behind me. Then, holding to the skirts of the woman before me, I groped my way up quickly—up and up through darkness with a close smell of bats in my nostrils—and almost before I could believe it, I stood with the panting, trembling group on the roof. The glare of the burning outhouses below shone on a great stack of chimneys beside us and reddened the sky above, and burnished the leaves of the chestnut trees that rose on a level with our eyes. But all the lower part of the steep roofs round us, and the lead gutters that ran between them, lay in darkness, the denser for the contrast. The flames crackled below, and a thick reek of smoke swept up past the coping, but the noise alike of fire and riot was deadened here. The night wind cooled our brows, and I had a minute in which to think, to breathe, to look round.

" Is there any other way to the roof? " I asked anxiously.

" One other, Monsieur! "

" Where? Or do you stay here, and guard this door," I said, pressing my gun on the man who had answered. " And let the boy come and show me. Mademoiselle, stay there, if you please."

The boy ran before me to the farther end of the roof, and in a lead walk, between two slopes, showed me a large trap-door. It had no fastening on the outside, and for a moment I stood nonplussed; then I saw, a few feet away, a neat pile of bricks, left there, I learned afterwards, in the course of some repairs. I began to remove them as fast as I could to the trap-door, and the boy saw and followed my example; in two minutes we had stacked a hundred and more on the door. Telling him to add another hundred to the number, I left him at the task and flew back to the women.

They might burn the house under us; that always, and for certain, and it meant a dreadful death. Yet I breathed more freely here. In the white and gold room below, among Madame's mirrors and Cupids, and silken cushions, and painted Venuses, my heart had failed me. The place, with its heavy perfumes, had stifled me. I had pictured the brutish peasants bursting in on us there—on the screaming women, crouching vainly behind chairs and couches; and the horror of the thought overcame me. Here, in the open, under the sky, we could at least die fighting. The depth yawned beyond the coping; the weakest had here no more to fear than death. Besides we had a respite, for the house was large, and the fire could not lick it up in a moment.

And help might come. I shaded my eyes from the light below, and looked into the darkness in the direction of the village and the Cahors road. In an hour, at furthest, help might come. The glare in the sky must be visible for miles; it would spur on the avengers. Father Benôit, too, if he could get help—he might be here at any time. We were not without hope.

Suddenly, while we stood together, the women sobbing and whimpering, the old man-servant spoke.

" Where is M. Gargouf? " he muttered under his breath.

" Ah! " I exclaimed; " I had forgotten him."

" He came up," the man continued, peering about him. " This door was open, M. le Vicomte, when we came to it."

" Ah! then where is he? "

I looked round too. All the roof, I have said, was dark, and not all of it was on the same level; and here and there chimneys broke the view. In the obscurity, the steward might be lurking close to us without our knowledge; or he might have thrown himself down in despair. While I looked, the boy whom I had left by the bricks came flying to us.

" There is someone there! " he said. And he clung to the old man in terror.

" It must be Gargouf! " I answered. " Wait here! "

And, disregarding the women's prayers that I would stay with them, I went quickly along the leads to the other trap-door, and peered about me through the gloom. For a moment I could see no one, though the light shining on the trees made it easy to discern figures standing nearer the coping. Presently, however, I caught the sound of someone moving; someone who was farther away still, at the very edge of the roof. I went on cautiously, expecting I do not know what; and close to a stack of chimneys I found Gargouf.

He was crouching on the coping in the darkest part, where the end wall of the east wing overlooked the garden by which I had entered. This end wall had no windows, and the greater part of the garden below it lay in darkness; the angle of the house standing between it and the burning buildings. I supposed that the steward had sneaked hither, therefore, to hide; and set it down to the darkness that he did not know me, but, as I approached, he rose on his knees on the ledge, and turned on me, snarling like a dog.

" Stand back ! " he said, in a voice that was scarcely human. " Stand back, or I will——"

" Steady, man," I answered quietly, beginning to think that fear had unhinged him. " It is I, M. de Saux."

" Stand back! " was his only answer; and, though he cowered so low that I could not get his figure against the shining trees, I saw a pistol-barrel gleam as he levelled it. " Stand back! Give me a minute! a minute only "—and his voice quavered—" and I will cheat the devils yet! Come nearer, or give the alarm, and I will not die alone! I will not die alone! Stand back! "

"Are you mad?" I said.

"Back, or I shoot!" he growled. "I will not die alone."

He was kneeling on the very edge, with his left hand against the chimney. To rush upon him in that posture was to court death; and I had nothing to gain by it. I stepped back a pace. As I did so, at the moment I did so, he slid over the edge and was gone.

I drew a deep breath and listened, flinching and drawing back involuntarily. But I heard no sound of a fall; and in a moment, with a new idea in my mind, I stepped forward to the edge, and looked over.

The steward hung in mid-air, a dozen feet below me. He was descending; descending foot by foot, slowly, and by jerks; a dim figure, growing dimmer. Instinctively I felt about me; and in a second laid my hand on the rope by which he hung. It was secured round the chimney. Then I understood. He had conceived this way of escape, perhaps had stored the rope for it beforehand, and, like the villain he was, had kept the thought to himself, that his chance might be better, and that he might not have to give the first place to Mademoiselle and the women. In the first heat of the discovery, I almost found it in my heart to cut the rope, and let him fall; then I remembered that if he escaped, the way would lie open for others; and then, even as I thought this, into the garden below me, there shone a sudden flare of light, and a stream of a dozen rioters poured round the corner, and made for the door by which I had entered the house.

I held my breath. The steward, hanging below me, and by this time half-way to the ground, stopped, and moved not a limb. But he still swung a little this way and that, and in the strong light of the torches which the new-comers carried, I could see every knot in the rope, and even the trailing end, which, as I looked, moved on the ground with his motion.

The wretches, making for the door, had to pass within a pace of the rope, of that trailing end; yet it was possible that, blinded by the lights they carried, and their own haste and excitement, they might not see it. I held my breath as the leader came abreast of it; I fancied that he must see it. But he passed, and disappeared in the doorway. Three others passed the rope together. A fifth, then three more, two more; I began to breathe more freely. Only one remained—a woman, the same whose imprecations had greeted me on my appearance at the window. It was not likely that she would see it. She was running to overtake the others; she carried a flare in her right hand, so that the blaze came between her and the rope. And she was waving the light in a mad woman's frenzy, as she danced along, hounding on the men to the sack.

But, as if the presence of the man who had wronged her had over her some subtle influence—as if some sense, unowned by others, warned her of his presence, even in the midst of that babel and tumult—she stopped short under him, with her foot almost on the threshold. I saw her head turn slowly. She raised her eyes, holding the torch aside. She saw him!

With a scream of joy she sprang to the foot of the rope, and began to haul at it as if in that way she might get to him sooner; while she filled the air with her shrieks and laughter. The men, who had gone into the house, heard her, and came out again; and after them others. I quailed, where I knelt on the parapet, as I looked down and met the wolfish glare of their upturned eyes; what, then, must have been the thoughts of the wretched man taken in his selfishness—hanging there helpless between earth and heaven? God knows.

He began to climb upwards, to return; and actually ascended hand over hand a dozen feet. But he had been supporting himself for some minutes, and at that point his strength failed him. Human muscles could do no more. He tried to haul himself up to the next knot, but sank back with a groan. Then he looked at me. "Pull me up!" he gasped in a voice just audible. "For God's sake! For God's sake, pull me up!"

But the wretches below had the end of the rope, and it was impossible to raise him, even had I possessed the strength to do it. I told him so, and bade him climb—climb for his life. In a moment it would be too late.

He understood. He raised himself with a jerk to the next knot, and hung there. Another desperate effort, and he gained the next; though I could almost hear his muscles crack, and his breath came in gasps. Three more knots—they were about a foot apart—and he would reach the coping.

But as he turned up his face to me, I read despair in his eyes. His strength was gone; and while he hung there, the men began, with shouts of laughter, to shake the rope this way and that. He lost his grip, and, with a groan, slid down three or four feet; and again got hold and hung there—silent.

By this time the group below had grown into a crowd—a crowd of maddened beings, raving and howling, and leaping up at him as dogs leap at food; and the horror of the sight, though the doomed man's features were now in shadow, and I could not read them, overcame me. I rose to draw back—shuddering, listening for his fall. Instead, before I had quite retreated, a hot flash blinded me, and almost scorched my face, and, as the sharp report of a pistol rang out, the steward's body plunged headlong down—leaving a little cloud of smoke where I stood.

STANLEY J. WEYMAN—*The Red Cockade.*

A DESERT SCRAP

THREE young Englishmen, Michael ("Beau"), Digby, his twin brother, and John Geste, join the French Foreign Legion, and this passage describes their first experience of active service against the Touareg nomads of the Sahara. It is John who tells the story.

A DESERT SCRAP

WE were in touch with the enemy at last. At any moment we might be fighting for our lives. We were delirious with excitement.

At once our little force in the oasis and this Arab *harka* became a microcosm of the whole war, and our Lieutenant Debussy sent out a small reconnoitring force under Sergeant-Major Lejaune which should be to the strung-out battalion what the battalion was to the brigade at Douargala.

It was the good luck of our *escouade* to be selected for this duty, and within half an hour of the arrival of the *goumiers*, we were advancing *en tirailleur* in the direction from which they had come. Over the loose, hot sand we plodded, our scouts far in advance and our flankers far out to left and right.

"Are we the bait of a trap? Or would you call us the point of a spear?" said Michael, marching between Digby and me.

"Both," replied Digby, "a bit of meat on the end of a spear, say."

And I wondered how many of us would be bits of meat before nightfall.

Not that I felt in the least degree apprehensive or depressed. If I had to analyse and describe my feelings, I should say that beneath a strong sensation of pleasurable excitement was that undercurrent of slight nervous anxiety which one experiences before going in to bat, or when seated in a corner of the ring, awaiting the word " *Time* " at the beginning of a boxing contest.

I would not have been elsewhere for worlds, but at the same time I wondered what the smack of a bullet felt like, and how much chance a bayonet stood against the heavy sword or the lance of a charging Arab. . . .

There was no doubt about it that Sergeant-Major Lejaune knew his job, and I found myself wishing that he were not such a wholly hateful person.

I should have liked to admire him as much as I admired his military skill, and ability as a commander, and I began to understand how soldiers love a good leader when it is possible to do so.

One felt that nobody could have handled the situation with more grasp and certainty than he did, and that if any kind of catastrophe or disaster ensued, it would be owing to no fault in the ability, courage, and promptitude of Sergeant-Major Lejaune.

To watch him conducting operations that day, was to watch a highly skilled artisan using his tools with the deftness and certainty of genius.

On a low, flat-topped rocky hill, we halted and rested, all except Lejaune himself and the scouts whom he sent to various distant sand-hills and low rocky eminences which, while visible from the detachment, gave a wide range of vision in the supposed direction of the enemy.

Among others set to similar tasks, I was ordered to

watch one particular man and to report any movement on his part. I watched the tiny distant figure
through the shimmering heat haze, which danced over
the sand and stones, until my eyes ached and I was
forced, from time to time, to close them and cover them
with my hand.

Upon opening them after one of these brief rests,
which were absolutely necessary, I saw that he was
crawling back from his position. When below the sky-
line, he rose and ran, stooping for a short distance. He
then halted and signalled *" Enemy in sight."*

The moment that I had pointed him out to Corporal
Boldini, Lejaune was notified, and he sent a man named
Rastignac running to an eminence, well to our left rear,
and a minute later we were lining the edge of our
plateau on the side to which this man had disappeared.

Here we lay concealed, and waited.

A few minutes later, the man who had been sent off,
fired a shot and exposed himself on the highest point
of his rocky hillock.

To my surprise, I saw our scouts retiring and running—not back to us, but to him; and, a minute or two
later, I saw a flutter of white on a distant sand-hill.

Rallying on the man who was firing from the top of
the rock, the scouts opened fire at distant camel-mounted
figures who began to appear over the sand-hills. We
received no orders, save to the effect that we should
lie as flat and still as the hot stones that concealed
us.

Between two of these I watched the scattered fringe
of Arabs increase to lines, and the lines to masses
of swiftly-moving camel-riders, and soon their deep

menacing cry of "*Ul-ul-ul-ul-ul-ullah Akbar,*" came to our ears like the growing roar of an advancing sea.

As they came on, the little party of our scouts fired rapidly, and after about the thousand-yard range, a camel would occasionally sprawl headlong to the ground, or a white-clad figure fall like a sack and lie motionless on the sand.

On swept the Arab *harka* at the top pace of their swift camels, the men in front firing from the saddle, the others brandishing their long, straight swords and waving their lances aloft.

Rapidly and steadily the little band of scouts fired into the brown of them, and, by now, every bullet was hitting man or beast in the closely-packed irregular ranks of the swiftly-advancing horde.

It was thrilling. I felt I must get a grip upon myself, or I should be shaking with excitement, and unable to shoot steadily when our turn came to take part in the fight.

And then, to my amazement, I saw that our scouts were retreating. One by one, they sprang up from behind rocks and fled to their right rear, each man dropping and firing as his neighbour rose to retreat in his turn. Before long, the little band was again in position, nearer to us and still further behind us. With increased yells, the Arabs swerved to their left and bore down upon them, men and camels falling beneath the magazine-fire of their rifles.

I could scarcely keep still. How long was this un-equal fight to continue? None of the scouts had been hit by the wild fire of the camel-riders, but in a couple of minutes they would be overwhelmed by this wave of mounted men, and, outnumbered by fifty to one, would have as much chance as has a fox beneath a pack of hounds.

And as I held my breath, the tiny handful again rose to their feet, turned their backs upon the Arabs, and fled as one man toward a sand-hill in our rear. With a simultaneous yell of mingled execration and triumph the Arab *harka* swerved again, seemed to redouble their speed, and bore down upon their prey.

And then, Sergeant-Major Lejaune stood up on a rock, gave a crisp order, coolly as on parade, and, at less than fifty yards, the Arab masses received the withering blast of our magazine fire.

Swiftly as our hands could move the bolts of our rifles and our fingers press the trigger, we fired and fired again into the surging, shrieking, struggling mob, that halted, charged, retired, and then fled, leaving quite half their number behind.

But of those who were left behind, by no means all were killed or even wounded, and our orgy of slaughter rapidly turned to a desperate hand-to-hand fight with dismounted and unwounded Arabs, who, knowing they must die, had but the one idea of gaining Paradise and the remission of sins, in the slaying of an infidel.

With a shout of "*Baïonnettes au canon*," Lejaune had us to our feet, and launched us in a fierce bayonet-charge down the slope of our plateau upon the Arab swordsmen, who were rallying to the attack, on foot. Our disciplined rush swept them back, they broke and fled, and, still keeping us in hand, Lejaune quickly had a double rank of kneeling and standing men shooting down the fleeing or still defiant foot-men, and making practice at the remains of the mounted *harka* disappearing over the skyline.

Within half an hour of the first signalling of the approach of the enemy, the only Arabs in sight were those that lay singly and in little bloodstained heaps, in the shallow valley into which they had been decoyed by our scouts.

It was a neat little action reflecting the highest credit on Lejaune and on the man who was the senior in charge of the scouts. The latter, one Gontran, was promoted corporal, in orders next day, and Sergeant-Major Lejaune made *adjudant*.

The Arabs must have lost over a hundred men in this fight, as against our three killed and five wounded.

Such was my first experience of war, my first " smelling of powder " and my blooding. I had killed a man with cold steel and I think at least three with my rifle.

Reflecting on this I was glad to remember that these Touaregs are human wolves, professional murderers, whose livelihood is robbery with violence which commonly takes the form of indescribable and unmentionable tortures.

Nor is the *Roumi*, the infidel dog, the favourite object of their treacherous attack, save in so far as he is a more rewarding object of attention. They are as much the scourge and terror of the Arab villager, the nomad herdsman, or the defenceless negro, as they are of the wealthy caravan or their peaceful co-religionists of the town, the *douar*, and the oasis.

The man whom I had killed with my bayonet, had made it necessary to my continued existence, for he rushed at me with a great, heavy, straight-bladed sword, exactly like those used by our Crusaders of old.

Whirling this round his head, he aimed a blow at me that would have split my skull had I not promptly side-stepped, drawing back my bayonet as I did so. As the sword missed my head, I drove at his chest with all my strength, and the curved hilt of my Lebel bayonet touched his breast-bone as he fell staggering back, nearly pulling the rifle out of my hands.

I found afterwards that Digby had his coat torn under the armpit by a spear, which, as he remarked, was not fair wear, but tear, on a good coat. He had shot his assailant at a range which he estimated as being a good half-inch, and he was troubled with doubts as to whether this would be considered quite sporting in the best Arab circles.

" Of course," he said, " the bird wasn't actually ' sitting ' —though he's sitting now. . . ."

Michael, being particularly good with the bayonet, and a noted winner of bayonet v. bayonet competitions, had used the butt of his rifle in the mêlée, and seemed to think it unfair of the Arab to wear a turban, that diminishes the neat effectiveness of this form of fighting! However, neither of them was hurt, nor were any of our more immediate friends.

Having buried our dead and obliterated their graves, we retired slowly toward El Rasa, weary to death and thoroughly pleased with ourselves, to make our report. . . .

P. C. WREN—*Beau Geste.*

SARACEN AND CRUSADER

THIS is the opening chapter of *The Talisman*, a tale of the Crusades. When King Richard fell ill, one of his knights was sent to consult a famous hermit, and on his way he encountered the unknown Saracen. The Knight of the Leopard was the son of the Scottish king and the unknown Saracen was the famous Saladin.

SARACEN AND CRUSADER

THE burning sun of Syria had not yet attained its highest point in the horizon, when a knight of the Red Cross, who had left his distant Northern home and joined the host of the Crusaders in Palestine, was pacing slowly along the sandy deserts which lie in the vicinity of the Dead Sea, or, as it is called, the Lake Asphaltites, where the waves of the Jordan pour themselves into an inland sea, from which there is no discharge of waters.

The warlike pilgrim had toiled among cliffs and precipices during the earlier part of the morning; more lately, issuing from those rocky and dangerous defiles, he had entered upon that great plain, where the accursed cities provoked, in ancient days, the direct and dreadful vengeance of the Omnipotent.

The toil, the thirst, the dangers of the way were forgotten, as the traveller recalled the fearful catastrophe which had converted into an arid and dismal wilderness the fair and fertile valley of Siddim, once well watered, even as the Garden of the Lord, now a parched and blighted waste, condemned to eternal sterility.

Crossing himself, as he viewed the dark mass of rolling waters, in colour as in quality unlike those of every other lake, the traveller shuddered as he remembered that beneath these sluggish waves lay the once proud cities of the plain, whose grave was dug by the

thunder of the heavens, or the eruption of subterrane-
ous fire, and whose remains were hid, even by that sea
which holds no living fish in its bosom, bears no skiff
in its surface, and, as if its own dreadful bed were the
only fit receptacle for its sullen waters, sends not, like
other lakes, a tribute to the ocean. The whole land
round, as in the days of Moses, was " brimstone and
d salt; it is not sown, nor beareth, nor any grass
groweth thereon " ; the land as well as the lake might
be termed dead, as producing nothing having resem-
blance to vegetation; and even the very air was entirely
devoid of its ordinary winged inhabitants, deterred
probably by the odour of bitumen and sulphur, which
the burning sun exhaled from the waters of the lake
in steaming clouds, frequently assuming the appearance
of waterspouts. Masses of the slimy and sulphurous
substance called naphtha, which floated idly on the
sluggish and sullen waves, supplied those rolling clouds
with new vapours, and afforded awful testimony to the
truth of the Mosaic history.

Upon this scene of desolation the sun shone with
almost intolerable splendour, and all living nature
seemed to have hidden itself from the rays, excepting
the solitary figure which moved through the flitting
and at a foot's pace, and appeared the sole breathing
thing on the wide surface of the plain. The dress of
the rider and the accoutrements of his horse were
peculiarly unfit for the traveller in such a country. A
coat of linked mail, with long sleeves, plated gauntlets,
and a steel breastplate, had not been esteemed a sufficient weight of armour; there was also his triangular
shield suspended round his neck, and his barred helmet

of steel, over which he had a hood and collar of mail
which was drawn around the warrior's shoulders
and throat, and filled up the vacancy between the
hauberk and the head-piece. His lower limbs were
sheathed, like his body, in flexible mail, securing the
legs and thighs, while the feet rested in plated shoes
which corresponded with the gauntlets. A long, broad
straight-shaped, double-edged falchion, with a handle
formed like a cross, corresponded with a stout poniard
on the other side. The knight also bore, secured to
his saddle, with one end resting on his stirrup, the long
steel-headed lance, his own proper weapon, which, as
he rode, projected backwards, and displayed its little
pennoncelle, to dally with the faint breeze, or drop in
the dead calm. To this cumbrous equipment must be
added a surcoat of embroidered cloth, much frayed
and worn, which was thus far useful, that it excluded
the burning rays of the sun from the armour, which
they would otherwise have rendered intolerable to the
wearer. The surcoat bore, in several places, the arms
of the owner, although much defaced. These seemed
to be a couchant leopard, with the motto, " I sleep—
wake me not." An outline of the same device might
be traced on his shield, though many a blow had almost
effaced the painting. The flat top of his cumbrous
cylindrical helmet was unadorned with any crest. In
retaining their own unwieldy defensive armour, the
Northern Crusaders seemed to set at defiance the nature
of the climate and country to which they had come to
war.

The accoutrements of the horse were scarcely less
massive and unwieldy than those of the rider. The

animal had a heavy saddle plated with steel, uniting
in front with a species of breastplate, and behind with
defensive armour made to cover the loins. Then there
was a steel axe, or hammer, called a mace-of-arms, and
which hung to the saddle-bow; the reins were secured
by chain-work, and the front-stall of the bridle was a
steel plate, with apertures for the eyes and nostrils,
having in the midst a short, sharp pike, projecting from
the forehead of the horse like the horn of the fabulous
unicorn.

But habit had made the endurance of this load of
panoply a second nature, both to the knight and his
gallant charger. Numbers, indeed, of the Western
warriors who hurried to Palestine died ere they became
inured to the burning climate; but there were others
to whom that climate became innocent and even
friendly, and among this fortunate number was the
solitary horseman who now traversed the border of
the Dead Sea.

Nature, which cast his limbs in a mould of un-
common strength, fitted to wear his linked hauberk
with as much ease as if the meshes had been formed
of cobwebs, had endowed him with a constitution as
strong as his limbs, and which bade defiance to almost
all changes of climate, as well as to fatigue and priva-
tions of every kind. His disposition seemed, in some
degree, to partake of the qualities of his bodily frame;
and as the one possessed great strength and endurance,
united with the power of violent exertion, the other,
under a calm and undisturbed semblance, had much
of the fiery and enthusiastic love of glory which con-
stituted the principal attribute of the renowned Norman

line, and had rendered them sovereigns in every corner of Europe where they had drawn their adventurous swords.

It was not, however, to all the race that fortune proposed such tempting rewards; and those obtained by the solitary knight during two years' campaign in Palestine had been only temporal fame, and, as he was taught to believe, spiritual privileges. Meantime, his slender stock of money had melted away, the rather that he did not pursue any of the ordinary modes by which the followers of the Crusade condescended to recruit their diminished resources at the expense of the people of Palestine; he exacted no gifts from the wretched natives for sparing their possessions when engaged in warfare with the Saracens, and he had not availed himself of any opportunity of enriching himself by the ransom of prisoners of consequence. The small train which had followed him from his native country had been gradually diminished, as the means of maintaining them disappeared, and his only remaining squire was at present on a sick-bed, and unable to attend his master, who travelled, as we have seen, singly and alone. This was of little consequence to the Crusader, who was accustomed to consider his good sword as his safest escort, and devout thoughts as his best companion.

Nature had, however, her demands for refreshment and repose, even on the iron frame and patient disposition of the Knight of the Sleeping Leopard; and at noon, when the Dead Sea lay at some distance on his right, he joyfully hailed the sight of two or three palm-trees, which arose beside the well which was assigned for his midday station. His good horse, too, which had plodded forward with the steady endurance of his master, now lifted his head, expanded his nostrils, and quickened his pace, as if he snuffed afar off the living waters, which marked the place of repose and refreshment. But labour and danger were doomed to intervene ere the horse or horseman reached the desired spot.

As the Knight of the Couchant Leopard continued to fix his eyes attentively on the yet distant cluster of palm-trees, it seemed to him as if some object was moving among them. The distant form separated itself from the trees, which partly hid its motions, and advanced towards the knight with a speed which soon showed a mounted horseman, whom his turban, long spear, and green caftan floating in the wind, on his nearer approach, showed to be a Saracen cavalier. " In the desert," saith an Eastern proverb, " no man meets a friend." The Crusader was totally indifferent whether the infidel, who now approached on his gallant barb, as if borne on the wings of an eagle, came as friend or foe—perhaps, as a vowed champion of the Cross, he might rather have preferred the latter. He disengaged his lance from his saddle, seized it with the right hand, placed it in rest with its point half elevated, gathered up the reins in the left, waked his horse's mettle with the spur, and prepared to encounter the stranger with the calm self-confidence belonging to the victor in many contests.

The Saracen came on at the speedy gallop of an Arab horseman, managing his steed more by his limbs and the inflection of his body than by any use of the reins, which hung loose in his left hand; so that he was enabled to wield the light round buckler of the skin of the rhinoceros, ornamented with silver loops, which he wore on his arm, swinging it as if he meant to oppose its slender circle to the formidable thrust of the Western lance. His own long spear was not couched or levelled like that of his antagonist, but grasped by the middle with his right hand, and brandished at arm's length above his head. As the cavalier approached his enemy at full career, he seemed to expect that the Knight of the Leopard should put his horse to the gallop to encounter him. But the Christian knight, well acquainted with the customs of Eastern warriors, did not mean to exhaust his good horse by any unnecessary exertion; and, on the contrary, made a dead halt, confident that, if the enemy advanced to the actual shock, his own weight, and that of his powerful charger, would give him sufficient advantage, without the additional momentum of rapid motion. Equally sensible and apprehensive of such a probable result, the Saracen cavalier, when he had approached towards the Christian within twice the length of his lance, wheeled his steed to the left with inimitable dexterity, and rode twice round his antagonist, who, turning without quitting his ground, and presenting his front constantly to his enemy, frustrated his attempts to attack him on an unguarded point; so that the Saracen, wheeling his horse, was fain to retreat to the distance of a hundred yards. A second time, like a hawk attacking a heron, the heathen renewed the charge, and a second time was fain to retreat without coming to a close struggle. A third time he

approached in the same manner, when the Christian
knight, desirous to terminate this elusory warfare, in
which he might at length have been worn out by the
activity of his foeman, suddenly seized the mace which
hung at his saddle-bow, and, with a strong hand and
unerring aim, hurled it against the head of the Emir,
for such and not less his enemy appeared. The Saracen
was just aware of the formidable missile in time to
interpose his light buckler betwixt the mace and his
head; but the violence of the blow forced the buckler
down on his turban, and though that defence also con-
tributed to deaden its violence, the Saracen was beaten
from his horse. Ere the Christian could avail himself
of this mishap, his nimble foeman sprung from the
ground, and calling on his steed, which instantly
returned to his side, he leaped into his seat without
touching the stirrup, and regained all the advantage of
which the Knight of the Leopard hoped to deprive
him. But the latter had in the meanwhile recovered
his mace, and the Eastern cavalier, who remembered
the strength and dexterity with which his antagonist
had aimed it, seemed to keep cautiously out of reach
of that weapon, of which he had so lately felt the force,
while he showed his purpose of waging a distant warfare with missile weapons of his own. Planting his long
spear in the sand at a distance from the scene of combat,
he strung, with great address, a short bow which he
carried at his back, and, putting his horse to the gallop,
once more described two or three circles of a wider
extent than formerly, in the course of which he dis-
charged six arrows at the Christian with such unerring
skill that the goodness of his harness alone saved him

from being wounded in as many places. The seventh shaft apparently found a less perfect part of the armour, and the Christian dropped heavily from his horse. But what was the surprise of the Saracen, when, dismounting to examine the condition of his prostrate enemy, he found himself suddenly within the grasp of the European, who had had recourse to this artifice to bring his enemy within his reach! Even in this deadly grapple the Saracen was saved by his agility and presence of mind. He unloosed the sword-belt, in which the Knight of the Leopard had fixed his hold, and, thus eluding his fatal grasp, mounted his horse, which seemed to watch his motions with the intelligence of a human being, and again rode off. But in the last encounter the Saracen had lost his sword and his quiver of arrows, both of which were attached to the girdle which he was obliged to abandon. He had also lost his turban in the struggle. These disadvantages seemed to incline the Moslem to a truce: he approached the Christian with his right hand extended, but no longer in a menacing attitude.

"There is truce betwixt our nations," he said, in the lingua franca commonly used for the purpose of communication with the Crusaders; "wherefore should there be war betwixt thee and me? Let there be peace betwixt us."

"I am well contented," answered he of the Couchant Leopard; "but what security dost thou offer that thou wilt observe the truce?"

"The word of a follower of the Prophet was never broken," answered the Emir. "It is thou, brave Nazarene, from whom I should demand security, did

I not know that treason seldom dwells with courage."

The Crusader felt that the confidence of the Moslem made him ashamed of his own doubts.

"By the cross of my sword," he said, laying his hand on the weapon as he spoke, "I will be true companion to thee, Saracen, while our fortune wills that we remain in company together."

"By Mahommed, Prophet of God, and by Allah, God of the Prophet," replied his late foeman, "there is not treachery in my heart towards thee. And now wend we to yonder fountain, for the hour of rest is at hand, and the stream had hardly touched my lip when I was called to battle by thy approach."

The Knight of the Couchant Leopard yielded a ready and courteous assent; and the late foes, without an angry look, or gesture of doubt, rode side by side to the little cluster of palm-trees.

SIR WALTER SCOTT *The Talisman.*

ENGLISH MASTIFFS

THIS is a story of the days of Queen Elizabeth. Amyas Leigh, his brother Frank, and their friend, Will Cary, fitted out the *Rose* and sailed to the Spanish Main. In an adventure at La Guayra Amyas barely escaped with his life, but Frank was left behind in the hands of the enemy.

ENGLISH MASTIFFS

When the sun leaped up the next morning, and the tropic night flashed suddenly into the tropic day, Amyas was pacing the deck, with dishevelled hair and torn clothes, his eyes red with rage and weeping, his heart full—how can I describe it? Picture it to yourselves, picture it to yourselves, you who have ever lost a brother, and you who have not, thank God that you know nothing of his agony. Full of impossible projects, he strode and staggered up and down, as the ship thrashed close-hauled through the rolling seas. He would go back and burn the villa. He would take Guayra, and have the life of every man in it in return for his brother's. " We can do it, lads! " he shouted. "If Drake took Nombre de Dios, we can take La Guayra." And every voice shouted, " Yes."

" We will have it, Amyas, and have Frank too, yet," cried Cary; but Amyas shook his head. He knew, and knew not why he knew, that all the ports in New Spain would never restore to him that one beloved face.

" Yes, he shall be well avenged. And look there! There is the first crop of our vengeance." And he pointed toward the shore, where, between them and the now distant peaks of the Silla, three sails appeared, not five miles to windward.

" There are the Spanish bloodhounds on our heels,

the same ships which we saw yesterday off Guayra, a big ship and two galleys. Back, lads, and welcome them, if they were a dozen."

There was a murmur of applause from all around, and if any young heart sank for a moment at the prospect of fighting three ships at once, it was awed into silence by the cheer which rose from all the older men, and by Salvation Yeo's stentorian voice.

" If there were a dozen, the Lord is with us, who has said, ' One of you shall chase a thousand.' Clear away, lads, and see the glory of the Lord this day."

" Amen! " cried Cary; and the ship was kept still closer to the wind.

The Spaniard, who had been coming upon them right down the wind under a press of sail, took in his light canvas.

" He don't know what to make of our waiting for him so bold," said the helmsman.

" He does, though, and means to fight us," cried another. " See, he is hauling up the foot of his mainsail: but he wants to keep the wind of us."

" Let him try, then," quoth Amyas. " Keep her closer still. Let no one fire till we are about. Man the starboard guns; to starboard and wait, all small-arm men. Pass the order down to the gunner, and bid all fire high, and take the rigging."

Bang went one of the Spaniard's bow-guns, and the shot went wide. Then another and another, while the men fidgeted about, looked at the priming of their muskets, and loosened their arrows in the sheaf.

" Lie down, men, and sing a psalm. When I want you, I'll call you. Closer still, if you can, helmsman, and we will try a short ship against a long one. We can sail two points nearer the wind than he."

As Amyas had calculated, the Spaniard would gladly enough have stood across the *Rose's* bows, but knowing the English readiness, dare not for fear of being raked; so her only plan, if she did not intend to shoot past her foe down to leeward, was to put her head close to the wind, and wait for her on the same tack.

Amyas laughed to himself. "Hold on yet awhile. More ways of killing a cat than choking her with cream. Drew, there, are your men ready?"

"Ay, ay, sir!" and on they went, closing fast with the Spaniard, till within a pistol-shot.

"Ready about!" and about she went like an eel, and ran upon the opposite tack right under the Spaniard's stern. The Spaniard, astounded at the quickness of the manœuvre, hesitated a moment, and then tried to get about also, as his only chance; but it was too late, and while his lumbering length was still hanging in the wind's eye, Amyas's bowsprit had all but scraped his quarter, and the *Rose* passed slowly across his stern at ten yards' distance.

"Now then!" roared Amyas. "Fire, and with a will! Have at her, archers: have at her, muskets all!" and in an instant a storm of bar and chain-shot, round and canister, swept the proud Don from stem to stern, while through the white cloud of smoke the musket-balls, and the still deadlier cloth-yard arrows, whistled and rushed upon their venomous errand. Down went the steersmen, and every soul who manned the poop. Down went the mizen top-mast, in went the stern-windows and the quarter-galleries; and as the smoke cleared away, the gorgeous painting of the *Madre Dolorosa*, with her heart full of seven swords, which, in a gilded frame, bedizened the Spanish stern, was shivered in splinters; while, most glorious of all, the golden flag of Spain, which the last moment flaunted above their heads, hung trailing in the water. The ship, her tiller shot away, and her helmsman killed, staggered helplessly a moment, and then fell up into the wind.

" Well done, men of Devon! " shouted Amyas, as cheers rent the welkin.

" She has struck," cried some, as the deafening hurrahs died away.

" Not a bit," said Amyas. " Hold on, helmsman, and leave her to patch her tackle, while we settle the galleys."

On they shot merrily, and long ere the armada could get herself to rights again, were two good miles to windward, with the galleys sweeping down fast upon them.

And two venomous-looking craft they were, as they shot through the short chopping sea upon some forty oars apiece, stretching their long sword-fish snouts over the water, as if snuffing for their prey. Behind this long snout, a strong square forecastle was crammed with soldiers, and the muzzles of cannon grinned out through port-holes, not only in the sides of the forecastle, but forward in the line of the galley's course, thus enabling her to keep up a continual fire on a ship right ahead.

The long low waist was packed full of the slaves, some five or six to each oar, and down the centre,

between the two banks, the English could see the slave-
drivers walking up and down a long gangway, whip in
hand. A raised quarter-deck at the stern held more
soldiers, the sunlight flashed merrily upon their armour
and their gun-barrels; as they neared, the English could
hear plainly the cracks of the whips, and the yells as
of wild beasts which answered them; the roll and rattle
of the oars, and the loud " Ha! " of the slaves which
accompanied every stroke, and the oaths and curses of
the drivers; while a sickening musky smell, as of a pack
of kennelled hounds, came down the wind from off
those dens of misery. No wonder if many a young
heart shuddered, as it faced, for the first time, the
horrible reality of those floating hells, the cruelties
whereof had rung so often in English ears, from the
stories of their own countrymen, who had passed them,
fought them, and now and then passed years of misery
on board of them. Who knew but what there might
be English among those sun-browned, half-naked
masses of panting wretches?

" Must we fire upon the slaves? " asked more than
one, as the thought crossed him.

Amyas sighed.

" Spare them all you can, in God's name; but if they
try to run us down, rake them we must, and God
forgive us."

The two galleys came on abreast of each other, some
forty yards apart. To outmanœuvre their oars as he
had done the ship's sails, Amyas knew was impossible.
To run from them, was to be caught between them and
the ship.

He made up his mind, as usual, to the desperate game.

173

"Lay her head up in the wind, helmsman, and we will wait for them."

They were now within musket-shot, and opened fire from their bow-guns; but owing to the chopping sea, their aim was wild. Amyas, as usual, withheld his fire.

The men stood at quarters with compressed lips, not knowing what was to come next. Amyas, towering motionless on the quarter-deck, gave his orders calmly and decisively. The men saw that he trusted himself, and trusted him accordingly.

The Spaniards, seeing him wait for them, gave a shout of joy—was the Englishman mad? And the two galleys converged rapidly, intending to strike him full, one on each bow.

They were within forty yards—another minute, and the shock would come. The Englishman's helm went up, his yards creaked round, and gathering way, he plunged upon the larboard galley.

"A dozen gold nobles to him who brings down the steersman!" shouted Cary, who had his cue.

And a flight of arrows from the forecastle rattled upon the galley's quarter-deck.

Hit or not hit, the steersman lost his nerve, and shrank from the coming shock. The galley's helm went up to port, and her beak slid all but harmless along Amyas's bow; a long dull grind, and then loud crack on crack, as the *Rose* sawed slowly through the banks of oars from stem to stern, hurling the wretched slaves in heaps upon each other; and ere her mate on the other side could swing round, to strike him in his new position, Amyas's whole broadside, great and small, had been poured into her at pistol-shot, answered by a yell which rent their ears and hearts.

"Spare the slaves! Fire at the soldiers!" cried Amyas; but the work was too hot for much discrimination; for the larboard galley, crippled but not undaunted, swung round across his stern, and hooked herself venomously on to him.

It was a move more brave than wise; for it prevented the other galley from returning to the attack without exposing herself a second time to the English broadsides; and a desperate attempt of the Spaniards to board at once through the stern-ports and up the quarter was met with such a demurrer of shot and steel, that they found themselves in three minutes again upon the galley's poop, accompanied, to their intense disgust, by Amyas Leigh and twenty English swords.

Five minutes' hard cutting, hand to hand, and the poop was clear. The soldiers in the forecastle had been able to give them no assistance, open as they lay to the arrows and musketry from the *Rose's* lofty stern. Amyas rushed along the central gangway, shouting in Spanish, "Freedom to the slaves! death to the masters!" clambered into the forecastle, followed close by his swarm of wasps, and set them so good an example how to use their stings, that in three minutes more, there was not a Spaniard on board who was not dead or dying.

"Let the slaves free!" shouted he. "Throw us a hammer down, men. Hark! there's an English voice!"

There is indeed. From amid the wreck of broken oars and writhing limbs, a voice is shrieking in broadest

Devon to the master, who is looking over the side.

" Oh, Robert Drew! Robert Drew! Come down, and take me out of hell! "

" Who be you, in the name of the Lord? "

" Don't you mind William Prust, that Captain Hawkins left behind in the Honduras, years and years agone? There's nine of us aboard, if your shot hasn't put 'em out of their misery. Come down, if you've a Christian heart, come down! "

Utterly forgetful of all discipline, Drew leaps down, hammer in hand, and the two old comrades rush into each other's arms.

Hardly were the decks cleared afresh, and the damage repaired as best it could be, when the Spanish ship came ranging up to leeward, as closehauled as she could.

She was, as I said, a long, flush-decked ship of full five hundred tons, more than double the size, in fact, of the *Rose,* though not so lofty in proportion; and many a bold heart beat loud, and no shame to them, as she began firing away merrily, determined as all well knew, to wipe out in English blood the disgrace of her late foil.

" Never mind, my merry masters," said Amyas, " she has quantity and we quality."

" That's true," said one, " for one honest man is worth two rogues."

" And one culverin three of their footy little ordnance," said another. " So when you will, Captain, and have at her."

" Let her come abreast of us, and don't burn powder. We have the wind, and can do what we like with her.

Serve the men out a horn of ale all around, steward, and all take your time."

So they waited for five minutes more, and then set to work quietly, after the fashion of English mastiffs, though, like those mastiffs they waxed right mad before three rounds were fired, and the white splinters (sight beloved) began to crackle and fly.

Amyas, having, as he had said, the wind, and being able to go nearer it than the Spaniard, kept his place at easy point-blank range for his two eighteen-pounder culverins which Yeo and his mate worked with terrible effect.

"We are hacking her through and through every shot," said he. "Leave the small ordnance alone yet awhile, and we shall sink her without them."

"Whing, whing," went the Spaniard's shot, like so many humming-tops, through the rigging far above their heads; for the ill-constructed ports of those days prevented the guns from hulling an enemy who was to windward, unless close alongside.

"Blow, jolly breeze," cried one, "and lay the Don over all thou canst. What the murrain is gone, aloft there?"

Alas! a crack, a flap, a rattle; and blank dismay! An unlucky shot had cut the fore-mast (already wounded) in two, and all forward was a mass of dangling wreck.

"Forward, and cut away the wreck!" said Amyas, unmoved. "Small-arm men be ready. He will be aboard of us in five minutes!"

It was too true. The *Rose*, unmanageable from the loss of her head-sail, lay at the mercy of the Spaniard;

and the archers and musketeers had hardly time to range themselves to leeward, when the *Madre Dolorosa's* chains were grinding against the *Rose's*, and grapples tossed on board from stem to stern.

"Don't cut them loose!" roared Amyas. "Let them stay and see the fun! Now, dogs of Devon, show your teeth, and hurrah for God and the Queen!"

And then began a fight most fierce and fell; the Spaniards, according to their fashion, attempting to board, the English, amid fierce shots of "God and the Queen!" "God and St. George for England!" sweeping them back by showers of arrows and musket balls, thrusting them down with pikes, hurling grenades and stink-pots from the tops; while the swivels of both sides poured their grape, and bar, and chain, and the great main-deck guns, thundering muzzle to muzzle, made both ships quiver and recoil, as they smashed the round shot through and through each other.

So they roared and flashed, fast clenched to each other in that devil's wedlock, under a cloud of smoke beneath the cloudless tropic sky; while all around, the dolphins gambolled, and the flying-fish shot on from swell to swell, and the rainbow-hued jellies opened and shut their cups of living crystal to the sun, as merrily as if man had never fallen, and hell had never broken loose on earth.

So it raged for an hour or more, till all arms were weary, and all tongues clove to the mouth. And sick men, rotting with scurvy, scrambled up on deck, and fought with the strength of madness; and tiny powder-boys, handing up cartridges from the hold, laughed and cheered as the shots rang past their ears; and old

Salvation Yeo, a text upon his lips, and a fury in his heart as of Joshua or Elijah in old time, worked on, calm and grim, but with the energy of a boy at play. And now and then an opening in the smoke showed the Spanish captain, in his suit of black steel armour, standing cool and proud, guiding and pointing, careless of the iron hail, but too lofty a gentleman to soil his glove with aught but a knightly sword-hilt: while Amyas and Will, after the fashion of the English gentleman, had stripped themselves nearly as bare as their own sailors, and were cheering, thrusting, hewing, and hauling, here, there, and everywhere, like any common mariner, and filling them with a spirit of self-respect, fellow-feeling, and personal daring, which the discipline of the Spaniards, more perfect mechanically, but cold and tyrannous, and crushing spiritually, never could bestow. The black-plumed señor was obeyed; but the golden-locked Amyas was followed; and would have been followed through the jaws of hell.

The Spaniards, ere five minutes had passed, poured *en masse* into the *Rose's* waist; but only to their destruction. Between the poop and forecastle (as was then the fashion), the upper-deck beams were left open and unplanked, with the exception of a narrow gangway on either side; and off that fatal ledge the boarders, thrust on by those behind, fell headlong between the beams to the main-deck below, to be slaughtered helpless in that pit of destruction, by the double fire from the bulk-heads fore and aft; while the few who kept their footing on the gangway, after vain attempts to force the stockades on poop and forecastle, leaped overboard again amid a shower of shot and arrows. The fire of the English was as steady as it was quick; and though three-fourths of the crew had never smelt powder before, they proved well the truth of the old chronicler's saying (since proved again more gloriously than ever, at Alma, Balaklava, and Inkermann) that "the English never fight better than in their first battle."

Thrice the Spaniards clambered aboard; and thrice surged back before that deadly hail. The decks on both sides were very shambles; and Jack Brimblecombe, who had fought as long as his conscience would allow him, found, when he turned to a more clerical occupation, enough to do in carrying poor wretches to the surgeon, without giving that spiritual consolation which he longed to give, and they to receive. At last there was a lull in that wild storm. No shot was heard from the Spaniard's upper-deck.

Amyas leaped into the mizen rigging, and looked through the smoke. Dead men he could descry through the blinding veil, rolled in heaps, laid flat; dead men and dying; but no man upon his feet. The last volley had swept the deck clear; one by one had dropped below to escape that fiery shower; and alone at the helm, grinding his teeth with rage, his mustachios curling up to his very eyes, stood the Spanish captain.

Now was the moment for the counter-stroke. Amyas shouted for the boarders, and in two minutes more he was over the side, and clutching at the Spaniard's mizen rigging.

What was this? The distance between him and the enemy's side was widening. Was she sheering off? Yes—and rising too, growing bodily higher every moment, as if by magic. Amyas looked up in astonishment; and saw what it was. The Spaniard was heeling fast over to leeward away from him. Her masts were all sloping forward, swifter and swifter—the end was come, then!

"Back! in God's name, back, men! She is sinking by the head!" And with much ado some were dragged back, some leapt back—all but old Michael Heard.

With hair and beard floating in the wind, the bronzed, naked figure, like some weird old Indian fakir, still climbed on steadfastly up the mizen-chains of the Spaniard, hatchet in hand.

"Come back, Michael! Leap while you may!" shouted a dozen voices. Michael turned,—

"And what should I come back for, then, to go home where no one knoweth me? I'll die like an Englishman this day, or I'll know the reason why!" and turning, he sprang in over the bulwarks, as the huge ship rolled up more and more, like a dying whale, exposing all her long, black bulk almost down to the keel, and one of her lower-deck guns, as if in defiance, exploded upright into the air, hurling the ball into the very heavens.

In an instant it was answered from the *Rose* by a column of smoke, and the eighteen-pound ball crashed through the bottom of the defenceless Spaniard.

"Who fired? Shame to fire on a sinking ship!"

"Gunner Yeo, sir," shouted a voice up from the main-deck. "He's like a madman down here."

"Tell him if he fires again, I'll put him in irons, if he were my own brother. Cut away the grapples aloft, men. Don't you see how she drags us over? Cut away, or we shall sink with her."

They cut away, and the *Rose*, released from the strain, shook her feathers on the wave-crest like a freed sea-gull, while all men held their breaths.

Suddenly the glorious creature righted herself; and rose again, as if in noble shame, for one last struggle with her doom. Her bows were deep in the water, but her after-deck still dry. Righted, but only for a moment, long enough to let her crew come pouring wildly up on deck, with cries and prayers, and rush aft to the poop, where, under the flag of Spain, stood the tall captain, his left hand on the standard-staff, his sword pointed in his right.

"Back, men!" they heard him cry, "and die like valiant mariners."

Some of them ran to the bulwarks, and shouted, "Mercy! We surrender!" and the English broke into a cheer, and called to them to run her alongside.

"Silence!" shouted Amyas. "I take no surrender from mutineers. Señor," cried he to the captain, springing into the rigging, and taking off his hat, "for the love of God and these men, strike! and surrender *à buena querra*."

The Spaniard lifted his hat, and bowed courteously, and answered, "Impossible, señor. No *querra* is good which stains my honour."

"God have mercy on you, then!"

"Amen!" said the Spaniard, crossing himself.

She gave one awful lunge forward, and dived under the coming swell, hurling her crew into the eddies. Nothing but the point of her poop remained, and there stood the stern and steadfast Don, cap-à-pie in his glistening black armour, immovable as a man of iron,

while over him the flag, which claimed the empire of
both worlds, flaunted its gold aloft and upwards in the
glare of the tropic moon.

"He shall not carry that flag to the devil with him;
I will have it yet, if I die for it!" said Will Cary, and
rushed to the side to leap overboard; but Amyas stopped
him.

"Let him die as he has lived, with honour."

A wild figure sprang out of the mass of sailors who
struggled and shrieked amid the foam, and rushed
upward at the Spaniard. It was Michael Heard. The
Don, who stood above him, plunged his sword into the
old man's body: but the hatchet gleamed, nevertheless:
down went the blade through head-piece and through
head; and as Heard sprang onward, bleeding, but alive,
the steel-clad corpse rattled down the deck into the
surge. Two more strokes, struck with the fury of a
dying man, and the standard-staff was hewn through.
Old Michael collected all his strength, hurled the flag
far from the sinking ship, and then stood erect one
moment, and shouted, "God save Queen Bess!" and
the English answered with a "hurrah!" which rent
the welkin.

Another moment, and the gulf had swallowed his
victim, and the poop, and him; and nothing remained
of the *Madre Dolorosa* but a few floating spars and
struggling wretches, while a great awe fell upon all
men, and a solemn silence, broken only by the cry:—

"Of some strong swimmer in his agony."

CHARLES KINGSLEY—*Westward Ho!*

NOTES

ROBERT LOUIS STEVENSON (1850-1894), poet, essayist, and novelist, was born at Edinburgh of a famous family of engineers and lighthouse builders. He studied law and was called to the Scottish Bar. But his health was always delicate and he needed to live an open-air life. He travelled in Europe and America, and ultimately settled in the South Sea island of Samoa, where he died. His first story was *Treasure Island;* then he produced *Dr. Jekyll and Mr. Hyde,* a mystery story of a dual personality; and afterwards the historical romances *Kidnapped,* its sequel *Catriona, The Black Arrow,* and *The Master of Ballantrae.* He also wrote several short stories, essays, and poems.

ALEXANDRE DUMAS (1802-1870) was one of the most popular and prolific of French writers. He made his reputation first as a dramatist and then turned to historical fiction. His best known stories are *The Three Musketeers* and *The Count of Monte Cristo.*

SIR HENRY RIDER HAGGARD (1856-1925) was born at Bradenham Hall, Norfolk. He was educated at Ipswich Grammar School and went to Natal as secretary to the Governor. Thereafter he served in various parts of South Africa. He afterwards travelled in many parts of the world and became an authority on Empire problems. He won his reputation as a novelist with *King Solomon's Mines,* which was first published in 1895. His other stories include *She, Ayesha* or *The Return of She, Allan Quatermain, Lysbeth,* and *Eric Brighteyes.*

JOHN JOY BELL (1871-1936) was born at Glasgow and educated at Glasgow University. He became a journalist and author, producing verses, plays, and stories. Of his plays, *Pie in Oven* was most successful, but it is by his study of the small Glasgow boy, *Wee Macgreegor,* that he is best known. He showed a fine command of descriptive prose in *The Whale Hunters* and *The Glory of Scotland.*

RICHARD DODDRIDGE BLACKMORE (1825-1900) was born at Longworth, Berkshire, and educated at Tiverton School and Exeter College, Oxford. Though trained to the Bar, he devoted himself to writing. He wrote many novels and poems, but his fame now rests on *Lorna Doone,* a romance of North Devon at the time of the Monmouth rebellion.

CHARLES DICKENS (1812-1870), one of our greatest novelists, was born at Landport, Portsmouth. When he was eleven years of age, the family removed to London. His father seems to have been a man like Mr. Micawber. Indeed, many of the characters and incidents of *David Copperfield* are based on Dickens' own early recollections. He had little schooling, worked for a time in a blacking factory, and then when the family finances improved, became a solicitor's clerk and afterwards a reporter. He won his first success as a writer with *The Pickwick Papers;* and thereafter he produced a new book almost every year until his death. He also travelled in Europe and America and gave public readings from his novels. He died in 1870 and was buried in Westminster Abbey.

As a novelist Dickens excelled in the creation of character rather than in the telling of a tale. We remember Mr. Pickwick and Sam Weller, Bob Cratchit and Tiny Tim, Ham, Emily and Peggotty, Paul Dombey, Little Nell and Oliver Twist as persons rather than as characters in a story. With his skill in characterization, Dickens reveals a humour that is peculiarly his own. Sometimes the humour is part and parcel of the character, as in the case of Sam Weller, whose every turn of thought and phrase is humorous, as if he looked upon the world with a twinkle in his eye. Sometimes the humour lies in situation, as when the staid Mr. Winkle attempts to skate, or when the artful waiter enjoys a substantial lunch at the expense of the solemn little boy that was David Copperfield.

HENRY SETON MERRIMAN (1862-1903) was the pen-name of Hugh Stowell Scott. He wrote many novels. He himself considered *Barlasch of the Guard* his best book, but *The Sowers, In Kedar's Tents,* and *Roden's Corner* are equally well known. His stories have all a European setting, being laid in such places as Russia, Poland, Spain, Corsica, Holland and France, and he visited all these places to get personal impressions.

DAVID WILLIAM BONE (born 1874) is a native of Glasgow. Entering the merchant service, he served in sailing-ships before he joined the Anchor Line. He is commander of R.M.S. *Transylvania.* His stories are of the sea, and among them are *The Brassbounder, Broken Stowage,* and *Capstan Bars.*

STANLEY JOHN WEYMAN (1855-1928) was born at Ludlow and educated at Shrewsbury and Christ Church, Oxford. He produced a long series of historical romances, many of them dealing with France, such as *A Gentleman of France, The House of the Wolf*, and *The Red Cockade*.

MAJOR PERCIVAL CHRISTOPHER WREN (born 1885) was educated at Oxford. He served in the French and Indian armies and in the French Foreign Legion. He made his name as a writer with *Beau Geste*, a tale of the Foreign Legion. It was followed by others such as *Beau Sabreur* and *Beau Ideal*. His latest books, *The Ghost of a Man* and its companion volume and sequel, *Worth Wile*, tell a story of the Indian Frontier.

SIR WALTER SCOTT (1771-1832) was born at Edinburgh. Most of his early boyhood was spent at Sandyknowe, his grandfather's Border farm, where he first heard and learned to love the old legends and tales of his native land. His father was a lawyer, and he himself was trained for law, called to the Scottish Bar, and became sheriff of Selkirkshire. Interested in the history and antiquities of Scotland, however, he spent much of his time in travelling the country, collecting ballads and tales, and in 1802 there appeared *Minstrelsy of the Scottish Border*, a collection of songs and ballads. His first original work was a long narrative poem, *The Lay of the Last Minstrel*, a tale of border feud. This was followed by *Marmion*, a tale of Flodden Field. Then came *The Lady of the Lake*, its story set in the Trossachs. In 1814 his first novel, *Waverley*, appeared, to be followed by the long series of novels now known as the Waverley Novels.

Scott's passionate interest in and deep knowledge of his-

188

tory provided the rich background of his stories. Kings, Princes, Lords and Ladies of high degree move freely in his pages, though he seldom succeeds in making these as real and vivid as the unforgettable Dugald Dalgetty, Dominie Sampson, Bailie Nicol Jarvie, or Jeanie Deans. He is not a humorist, as Dickens is, but kindly and genial himself, he has infused some of his own qualities into his stories. He sets his historical stage so elaborately in the opening chapters that especially to modern readers his stories appear slow to begin, but it is worth while to persevere, for Scott was pre-eminently a story-teller.

CHARLES KINGSLEY (1819-1875) was born in Devonshire and educated at Cambridge. He took orders and became curate and afterwards rector of Eversley, where he remained till his death. He was a man of wide interests and wrote on many subjects. Young readers usually make acquaintance with him first in his delightful fantasy, *The Water Babies*, and then in *The Heroes*, his rendering of three of the famous Greek myths. The best known of his novels are the historical tales, *Hereward the Wake* and *Westward Ho!*